Fire

PATRICIA WILSON

Heartline
Books

Published by Heartline Books Limited in 2001

Copyright © Patricia Wilson 2001

Patricia Wilson has asserted her rights under the copyright,
Designs and Patents Act, 1988 to be identified as the
author of this work.

First published in the United Kingdom in 2001
by Heartline Books Limited.

Heartline Books Limited
PO Box 22598, London W8 7GB

Heartline Books Ltd. Reg No: 03986653

ISBN 1-903867-11-8

Styled by Oxford Designers & Illustrators

Printed and bound in Great Britain by
Cox & Wyman, Reading, Berkshire

PATRICIA WILSON

Patricia Wilson is at her happiest when travelling about and looking at new places. Perhaps she has some gypsy blood because what is over the hill or around the next corner has always intrigued her. Patricia has lived in the Far East, Africa, France and Spain and has immersed herself in the sights and sounds of all these places to use in her writing. She likes old houses and loves to wander around them – peopling the houses with characters for a book. If she's in the right mood, in the right place, stories just come into her head and she has to write them!

At the moment Patricia lives in the Republic of Ireland which holds its own fascination with its legends and landscape, fairy hills and soft, unpredictable weather. She would dearly like to own an Irish Wolfhound but is not sure how her family would feel about sharing the house with a dog as big as a small pony, as they already tolerate her love of marmalade cats!

To relax, Patricia plays the piano, paints and watches murder films on television. She loves writing romantic fiction and says, 'I must confess that I never want to let the heroes go when I have created them. They are too real to me. I think the heroine is always some part of the writer but the hero is something else again. On second thoughts, to fill the house with big, handsome men and a huge dog is perhaps not a good idea!'

chapter one

Alissa glanced at her watch and then gave an exaggerated sigh. She was far too early and as Candy was always late for appointments, she clearly faced a long and irritating wait. Alissa was not much given to sitting around and gazing at strangers. She was not the sort of person who could sip an aperitif while relaxing in the company of people she didn't know and would never see again. She would rather be doing something.

She dived off to the right and was soon driving into an area she hadn't seen before. She had discovered a quiet road minutes away from the traffic. Astonished to find a place like this in the heart of the city, Alissa looked about her with interest. It was so peaceful, a haven of tranquillity in the chaotic excitement of London. It was astounding that she hadn't seen this place before and had only found it because she wanted to kill some time.

Her mobile phone rang and as it was in the bottom of her bag beside her on the passenger seat, there was no chance of quickly snatching it up. She drew up and parked at the side of the tree-lined road in no great hurry. She could guarantee the call would be from her sister, ringing to make sure that she'd remembered about their date for lunch.

'Are you on your way?' Candy's voice was motherly, anxious and fussing, which was normal.

'I'm just about to hit the traffic.'

'I wish you wouldn't use that expression. Just take care because there's plenty of time. No need to take any head-strong risks.'

Alissa suppressed her laughter as it bubbled up and threatened to escape. Headstrong? There was nothing headstrong about her. Coolly efficient was how she would have described herself. Fluffy-headed was how she thought of Candy.

Her sister was the perfect wife and mother. Marrying Bob and having his children had been her one dream for years. She did the things that happily married women do. She cooked wonderful meals, took care of her small family, took her turn in the car pool for school, attended parent meetings and was pretty as a picture when Bob came home at night.

Alissa thought it was all very nice, very boring and more than a little frightening. The Tender Trap with no room for adventure. She had no intention of walking into that velvet-lined prison herself. As far as she was concerned, men were extremely sneaky individuals, constantly on the lookout for someone to wash their shirts and make them a three-course meal.

She stopped paying too much attention when Candy launched into a long story about a neighbour. Apparently it had slipped her mind at the moment that they were supposed to be meeting for lunch. As usual this was something she *just had* to tell Alissa.

Candy was capable of holding a one-sided conversation and Alissa had learned to switch off when they were both children. She just had to appear to be listening and her sister would take it from there. Alissa had heard similar stories with improbable variations since Candy had become a proud house-owner and this seemed to be the usual excitement that happened outside the velvet prison.

Alissa shuddered and listened with no more than part of her attention.

A black Ford came slowly along the road, passing her. It

stopped a good way in front but Alissa merely glanced at it. Her eyes were turned to the rather grand area where she was parked.

Apart from her own car and the car in front, the road was deserted. Big houses, so silent they might well have been unoccupied, were set far back behind electronically controlled gates. Their huge gardens blended with the elegant curve of woodland. There were flowers and well-manicured lawns. Some had long drives and there was a feeling of well-guarded privacy to the whole area.

No other place in London could have retained this air of tranquillity on a sunny morning when the rest of the city hummed with frenzied activity. In this hushed place, with its restrained air of wealth, any noise, bustle and traffic seemed unthinkable. Alissa made a wry face. These houses belonged to the seriously rich who were probably stuffy and tedious.

She could imagine millionaires sitting down to solitary lunches, their cold eyes looking suspiciously at the soup.

Her imagination widened to take in downtrodden servants waiting to serve, hoping that cook had done the right things. No, it would be a chef. She adjusted her mental pictures, removed the homely cook and replaced her with a chef in a tall hat. She gave him a neat French moustache and felt sorry for him.

What a way to live, when outside the sun was shining and birds were singing in the trees.

Two children stepped out through the gates of a little park. It was obviously a private park, strictly for the residents of this elegant, gilt-edged road because a young woman in a grey uniform lingered to lock the gates as they left.

Alissa watched them as Candy droned on and on. She made occasional sounds of astonishment or commiseration, where required, but her attention was on the children.

They were quite beautiful. The little girl was about five, her blonde curls shining in the sun. The boy was older. He must have been eight and his appearance contrasted with the girl's quite sharply. His hair was black and he looked very self-possessed.

As a teacher, Alissa was interested and she watched them walk up the road, the small girl's hand securely in the young woman's. A nanny, Alissa surmised. The children probably came from one of the big houses. That fact probably accounted for the boy's rather cool composure.

Candy had almost run out of words by now and was winding up her tale but Alissa's eyes still lingered on the children. The girls she taught were very much older than these two, but part of her mind was summing them up, wondering how the girl could be so sunny, skipping along beside the nanny while the boy walked along, stiffly silent.

In front of them, she saw the passenger door of the black Ford open. A man stepped out but immediately bent into the back of the car. Alissa didn't take much notice. He appeared to be busy, with the door wide open and obstructing the pavement. It was the kind of thoughtless thing she'd seen people do a hundred times.

The two children moved to step around the obstacle, the small party breaking into single file. It was all so natural and Alissa watched them with a smile still on her face. They were so beautifully dressed, so well behaved. Picture book children.

Suddenly the man leapt up and the boy was seized. He was flung along the back seat of the car to be held, struggling and kicking, by the driver.

Capturing the little girl was not so easy. The nanny was alerted. She began to scream and cling tightly to the child who was also screaming in a high-pitched voice. It was impossible to free her from the nanny's grip, especially as the boy joined in too.

'Kick, Sally! Bite!' His shouts echoed in the road as he struggled to stick his head out the car. He was pulled back inside and as a hand came round her mouth, the little girl bit hard. Small, sharp teeth sank into the hand that grasped her and the man let go as blood seeped to the surface.

'You little…!'

'Leave her!'

At the shouted order the man slammed the back door of the car and leapt into the passenger seat. The car roared away with the boy still inside, the driver now concentrating on the road. Behind them the little girl was still screaming. Tears were running down her face but the boy was captured.

Alissa had been too shocked to react. Everything had happened so fast that she hardly believed her eyes. Then she shouted, 'Got to go', threw the phone down and gunned her car into action.

She had just seen a kidnapping. She felt dazed, unbelieving, but every instinct told her to act and she acted. She sped past the nanny and screaming child and followed the kidnappers.

The Ford turned into the busy traffic that sped past on a larger road. The driver adjusted his speed and they were lost in the turbulent ferment of London at lunchtime.

The driver was pleased. One child was more than enough to handle and this was the one who counted. He ignored the boy because the speed was too great for any move to escape. In any case, the kid was too scared.

'That nanny saw me. Nobody saw you sitting there.'

As the man in the passenger seat began to grumble, the driver gave him an irritated glance. 'You're worrying about that when I've seen you smash a window and help yourself to the display? The kid will remember me all right but I'm not bothered. Tempest won't call the police. He'll pay. We give the kid back and it's all over. Pull yourself together.'

'You could have done the job. I could have been driving. There was a woman in a car there. She'll have spotted me too.'

'She was talking on the phone. When a woman gets talking on the phone she sees nothing.' Eyes filled with annoyance he glanced across. 'Now shut the hell up. You'll get paid more for this than you could earn in six months. It took ten minutes and it's over.'

Alissa followed in the busy traffic, praying they hadn't noticed her. She should phone the police but she was terrified the kidnappers would elude her and simply disappear. By the time they came to traffic lights, she had daringly dodged round a taxi and had horns blaring at her. She had run too close for comfort to a bus and managed to get past another car but she was right behind her target now.

The lights changed to red and as they stopped, Alissa, acting again by sheer intuition, leapt out of her car and raced forward. She yanked open the back door of the Ford and reached in for the boy.

She shouted, 'Quick. You're safe, I've got you. Come on!'

To her great relief he came at once, evading the startled men who tried to grab him and before the lights could change, she had him in her car with all the doors locked.

Everything had happened in a flurry and Alissa felt decidedly wobbly, her heart was hammering like a drum. She couldn't understand why the whole of the populace wasn't shouting at her and trying to intervene.

The men in the other car jumped out, then appeared to

think better of it. When the lights changed they pulled away and disappeared round the corner. Alissa was shaking with reaction, her legs felt like rubber but she made a daring turn across the traffic and headed back the way they had come. No black car was in pursuit and they were safe as far as she could tell.

'Thank you,' the boy said with astonishing composure.

Alissa glanced at him. He hadn't cried at all. His small handsome face was utterly calm – too calm. She wondered if he was in shock and made her voice seem normal.

'Don't mention it. A good deed every day. Dragons killed to order. Boys rescued with ease. It's all part of the service.'

'I suppose you're kidnapping me now?' His voice was quiet, resigned. He didn't even seem afraid and Alissa glanced at him again.

'No. It's not a kidnapping day for me,' she said cheerfully. 'I'm taking you back. What's your name?'

'James. My sister is called Sally.'

'I know. I heard you shouting to her. She's got quite a scream.'

'She's very small. Screaming is her only weapon against grown-ups.'

His choice of words seemed to indicate his opinion of grown-ups and Alissa was silent. Was this the result of living in a wealthy household? The girls she taught were from quite rich families but not one of them had the strange air of aloofness this child possessed. Not one of them could have been involved in a kidnap attempt and come out of it unruffled.

'Show me where you live,' Alissa ordered as they came once again to the quiet road. It was still as silent as before. She had almost expected police cars, some kind of activity, but everything had happened so fast. It was still unbelievable and unnerving as if she'd stepped into a dream.

'Here.' As she drew to a halt beside big wrought iron gates, he turned to look at her. 'Will you come in? My father will want to reward you.'

Alissa felt a sharp burst of annoyance. Why should anyone wish to reward her for simply doing her duty when the need arose? She didn't even want thanks. This child was showing no sign of any real emotion either. Being extremely rich seemed to have many hidden disadvantages. She remembered his stoic composure before and thought maybe he wasn't shocked but was always like this.

'No, thank you. I was glad to help. Are you quite sure this is where you live? I wouldn't want you to be grabbed again.'

'This is where I live.' He looked at her very steadily. 'And I won't be kidnapped again. My father won't allow it. Those men will be punished.'

Alissa stared at him in consternation. He could not be more than eight-years-old but he had a coolness about him that was astounding. She didn't understand his attitude at all. Perhaps it really was shock?

'I'll wait here until you're inside the gate.'

He nodded and climbed out of the car, standing by the door and looking back at her. 'I think you'd better tell me your name. My father will ask.'

And send her a diamond necklace through the post no doubt?

'Just call me Alissa. I don't have a business card on me at the moment but you can tell your father I slay dragons and other deadly beasts. I'm in the phone book under "Help Required".'

The little boy looked at her with no sign of amusement. 'I'll tell him.' He slanted her another curious look, gave a rather stately nod and walked to the gates. He dialled a number and went through them as they slowly opened.

Alissa watched as he walked up the tree-lined drive and the gates closed again. He looked small and rather pitifully lonely. Something about him touched her heart, even the way he kept his back straight was lonely, defensive.

She turned her car round and headed back to keep her appointment with Candy. She wouldn't tell her sister about this unexpected adventure and she wasn't sure what had startled her most, the kidnapping or the strange behaviour of the small boy. If she had ever wanted wealth this had changed her mind.

A little earlier, Kieran Tempest heard the front door being flung open and even before he heard the desolate cries he was on his feet, rounding the desk, with every sense alert to danger.

A child burst into the study and flung herself forward as soon as she saw him. 'They've got James! Somebody stole James, Daddy! A car took him away and Bessie couldn't get him back.'

He swept the weeping child up into his arms, his hand enclosing the little head of silky curls as his eyes turned on the young woman who came into the room with tears streaming down her face too.

'I couldn't help it, Mr Tempest. It was so quick. They just snatched James from the street.' She looked afraid, as if he would strike her down on the spot.

'Tell me. Every detail.'

'It was a black car, oldish. I think it was a Ford. I got the number, I wrote it on the dental appointment card from my pocket.'

He just held out his hand without a word and she moved forward anxiously, slipping the card into his hand and stepping back as fast as possible.

'Go on,' he said without expression. 'What else?'

'They tried to take them both. I got hold of James but when they tried to get Sally I had to let one of them go.'

'They grabbed my arm,' Sally sobbed. 'It still hurts.'

'Shh,' he murmured, tightening his arms around her. 'We'll fix it soon.' His eyes went back to the young nanny and she bit anxiously at her lips.

'They pulled away when they couldn't get them both. I shouted and screamed but it was too late. The car just drove off round the corner into the next road. There was another car too but I don't know if it was with them. It went by fast and I didn't get that number. I thought it best to come back and let you know. In any case, Sally was screaming and crying and…'

'Get her settled down. I'll be up to her soon. I'll phone the police.'

He handed the child over and looked at the card in his hand. By now they would probably have ditched the car and picked up another. Chances were slim. Pain, grief and fury burned in his mind.

'Will we get James back, Daddy?'

'Yes.' He bit out the word and then added more quietly, 'Yes, darling, we will. Go with Bessie and wash your face. Have a drink and I'll call the police. There's nothing to be afraid of. Nobody can touch you now and I'll get James back.'

He would get James back. He had not one single doubt about that but how long would it take and what damage would have been done to his son by then? There were plenty of people who would give their all to have some sort of hold on him. If they had James, they would have all the hold they needed, because he cared for nothing but his children. Anyone who knew anything about him was well aware of that.

Who had acted so swiftly, so determinedly? He would find out and then he would punish them savagely. There was coldness around his heart as he picked up the telephone to call the police.

As he was speaking on the phone, he heard the front door open again. This time there was no sound of crying or shouting but he recognised the footsteps, the dogged precision, and the controlled approach that was far too calm for a child. It was a child though – his child.

'I'll get back to you immediately.' He put the phone down and turned as the door to his study opened.

'I got away.'

Considering the shock, the trauma of the experience, the calm words were astonishing but Kieran Tempest was not astonished at all. He knew what went on in the mind of his son. He also knew not to move forward and clutch the child to him as his instincts dictated.

'I thought you might.' He walked to the leather settee and sat down, patting the seat beside him. 'Come and tell me about it.'

James came forward like a grown-up. 'Is Sally all right?'

'She's fine. A lot of tears but she's settled now. When you've told me what happened we'll go up and see her. She's worried about you.'

'It's not Bessie's fault. She tried but it was all planned. They must have been watching us.'

Kieran Tempest kept a tightly controlled expression on his face. He wanted to hug the boy to him, hold him close but he could not do that. James had decided a long time ago exactly what role he would play and so far he had never shown any sign of softening. Today's events would only make things worse.

'How did you get away?'

The child gave him a puzzled look. 'It was really peculiar. A strange lady drove up. She was beautiful but I thought she was a bit odd.'

'Why odd?' The new information was instantly catalogued in Kieran's brain.

'She was quick and really brave but she wouldn't tell me who she was except that her name was Alissa. She was a bit strange anyway. She said she killed dragons and other dangerous beasts for a living. That was an alibi I think because there are no dragons. I asked her to come in to meet you but she wouldn't. She said that if you wanted to get in touch with her she's in the telephone book under "Help Required". Who do you think she is?'

Kieran was intrigued by this information and at any other time he would have been highly amused, but he was thinking fast and already a plan was forming in his mind. As usual he kept it to himself.

'She was doing a good deed. Perhaps she just goes around doing good deeds.'

'That's what I thought. So I got her car number. It was a blue car. Does that help?'

'It does. Write it down before you forget it. You're very clever, James.'

The boy stood by Kieran's desk, writing the car number but sparing time to glance at his father. 'Most people are stupid though and Uncle Carl is more stupid than anyone.'

'I'm inclined to agree with you,' Kieran acknowledged, trying to hide the slight quirk to his hard mouth, 'but why pick on him at this particular time?'

'He was giving orders to the other man. He said it didn't matter about Sally because they'd got me. Uncle Carl was driving the car.'

'Was he really?' No sign of emotion showed on Kieran's

face but his eyes were glittering with icy satisfaction. 'That's very interesting.' He sat back comfortably. 'Now tell me all about this peculiar lady and how she rescued you. Don't miss anything out because I'm really intrigued.'

Later, when the children were settled, he rang the police and told them not to bother with any hunt. His son was back. He had a plan of his own and didn't need the police. What he did need, however, was the daring young woman who had rescued James. He set in motion the means of tracing her.

Two weeks later, Alissa had another luncheon date with her sister and looking at Candy closely, she suspected the main reason for it. She waited, knowing it would all be explained in great detail.

'You can live with us for the six months.'

Alissa suppressed a smile as her sister made this offer. She had been expecting it all day. The reason for the shopping trip and this rather expensive lunch had very quickly become clear as soon as Candy met her. Mother Hen was fluffing up her feathers.

'Not at all necessary. I'm not penniless. I'm healthy, strong and I have a roof over my head. Desperate action is out of the question and to live with you and Bob, I really would have to be very desperate.'

'But you can't take up your old job for six months,' Candy leaned forward to emphasise her point, keeping her voice low. 'What are you going to do in the meantime? You need money to keep that house on, to say nothing of the basic requirement of eating. No job, no wage, no money.'

'I thought of all that before I took time off to teach over-seas. I'm not exactly an idiot.' Alissa's dark eyes narrowed and she looked annoyed. 'Of course, I fully expected my job to be handed back to me when I was ready. The fact that they might offer a longer contract to the person who took over from me didn't enter my head.' She made a wry face. 'Apparently, the governors thought I would go native and refuse to come back to England. Still, it's only for six months and then I'm with my own girls again.'

'Bob thinks you should sue,' Candy muttered, finishing off her cheesecake with satisfaction.

'Fiddlesticks!' Alissa knew all about Bob's desire to sue anyone who blinked three times in the wrong place. It was amusing but he was not going to involve her.

'Well, this gets us no further forward,' Candy remarked, signalling briskly to the waiter for coffee. 'We think you should let the house go and come to us for the six months and then see what happens.'

'Oh, I know what will happen. You'll try to make me eat too much. You'll fuss over me until I scream and Bob will insist on driving me everywhere in case lunatics set upon me. I'm twenty-five! I've lived overseas for a year and survived very well. As to letting the house go, it took me months to find it and get the lease and it's only a few miles from school. I'd rather let the car go and walk everywhere.'

'Alissa!' Candy looked at her in horror. 'It's lonely there. You live so far away. Walking to school would be dangerous.'

'Let it go, Candy. I'm sticking to my plan. If you need someone to mother, then have another baby.'

'Three children are enough for anyone – Bob says.' Candy looked doubtful and Alissa smiled into her coffee. Candy was feeling maternal again, hence the need to mother and smother. At least her own remarks about children had thrown her sister off the scent somewhat. Candy's eyes had gone all vacant-looking.

'What a gorgeous man!' Candy whispered suddenly,

adding in a low hiss, 'No, don't look round now. He's at that table by the window. I bet he's a film star.'

'You're a married lady.' Alissa never looked round. Candy was always imagining she saw film stars, somebody who looked like one of them, some film star in disguise so as not to be noticed.

'I'm only looking! Being married hasn't made me blind.' She gave Alissa all her attention again however. 'So what about money? If you insist on being alone, we'll have to help you.'

'I knew I shouldn't have agreed to meet you,' Alissa sighed. 'Stop worrying about me. It's all taken care of. With a bit of luck, I'll have a job for six months before I even get back today.'

'You could have told me that right away!' Candy sat up and looked indignant. 'You let me have all that worry for nothing. What sort of job?' She didn't bother to hide her suspicion.

'I put my name down with an agency and something came up.'

'You're *not* going to clean houses?' Candy gave a horrified gasp and Alissa looked at her with resigned pity.

'Of course I'm not. I'm going to act as a tutor until my own job is vacant again. It's the obvious solution. Most jobs like that are live-in, meals supplied and pretty fair wages. I've got an appointment this afternoon.' She glanced at her watch. 'In one hour actually. It's just down the road from here.'

'I'm going with you. Whoever this person is who wants a tutor, they'll need inspecting. You could be molested. You can't even think of living in somebody's house. Why, it might just be a ruse to get you alone, in their power.'

'For heavens sake! I'm not going to get mixed up with

white slavers and nobody is going to get me in their power. I didn't answer an ad in the paper. This is a good agency. They inspect the clients and interview the applicants. I should know, they checked me pretty thoroughly. It threw the school governors into further panic as they thought I wasn't going back after all.'

'Which would serve them right. Your job should have been waiting for you. If you go off and never come back it will be all their fault.'

'Oh, I'll come back. I don't like my plans to be thwarted when I had it all worked out. This is just a temporary set back.'

'All the same,' Candy insisted, 'I'll come to this meeting with you. They'll be able to see then that you've got some-body to fight for you.'

Alissa looked at her sister's diminutive size and shook her head. This elusive 'they' would not be impressed. 'You will not go with me. I don't need you to hold my hand and that's the end of the matter, Candy. Now drink your coffee, then I can spare about fifteen minutes at that shop up the road. You wanted a new sweater, didn't you?'

Candy seemed to have run out of steam because she obeyed and once more her eyes turned to the window. 'You can glance round now,' she whispered. 'He's eating. He'll not see you.'

'Who?' Alissa looked mystified and Candy jerked her short blonde curls toward the other side of the room.

'That man I told you about. That gorgeous man.'

Alissa dutifully looked and her eyebrows rose in surprise. Bob Morris was a charming, smiling man and Candy worshipped him. This gorgeous man looked downright alarming. His face was too harsh, his hair was as black as a raven and he glanced up with piercingly grey eyes, giving

Alissa quite a nasty shock.

An expensive suit didn't do anything at all to disguise his menacing, savage aura. He looked dangerous, fierce and utterly forbidding. Just glancing at him was probably near fatal.

'Are you out of your mind?' She cradled her coffee cup in her hands, muttering into it just in case he was still looking her way and capable of reading her lips. 'He looks really dark and dangerous! I wouldn't like to meet *him* around a quiet corner on a moonless night.'

'I think he's handsome. Quite extraordinary.'

'Extraordinarily ferocious by the look of him. Stick with Bob.'

'Of course I'll stick with Bob! I was simply looking.'

'Well don't look again. Let's go before you get into trouble and don't try to take care of me until you've learned to take care of yourself. Bob should keep you locked up. Casting glances at a man like that is tantamount to risking foul play.'

'I just thought he looked unusual. You don't see many men like that.'

'And we should be eternally grateful. Icy-eyed predators are always unusual and we avoid them. This knowledge keeps me safe. *You* blunder into trouble. Let's go!'

They walked out and Candy scurried along at Alissa's side, quite unnerved by now. It brought a smile to Alissa's lips. She had never needed help herself. In fact, she was the one who had always kept an eye on her older sister. Even as children, Alissa had fought Candy's battles. She was taller, more alert and much more sceptical. Candy was not at all street-wise. She was pretty, cuddly and thought well of anyone who wasn't a danger to her family. Alissa had to fight to stay out of this snuggly warmth. Candy had the Mother Hen complex. She had probably been born with it.

They stepped into the street and Alissa never glanced back at the window although she was uncomfortably aware of the man behind the glass. The jungle was full of ferocious animals and staring fixedly at them was not recommended.

The fact that this one looked handsome, expensive and important didn't fool her one little bit. Far from being a film star, he looked like a hunter ready to go on the prowl. She took Candy's arm and hurried her off down the street, thankful when the restaurant was well out of sight.

chapter two

Later, as she waited in the luxurious reception area of the agency, Alissa tried to avoid looking too long at herself in the big gilt mirror that adorned one wall. The mirror was huge and she hoped it wasn't two-way, with the prospective employer watching from the other side while hopeful applicants inspected themselves for faults. Anxiety was a new experience to Alissa and she wondered where this sudden quivering in her stomach had come from?

Like her sister she was fair, but she didn't have the same short blonde, bouncy curls. Her hair was heavy, long, swept back from her face and falling to her shoulders in a shining, golden curtain that caught the light. Her brown eyes were large, edged with thick black lashes and her finely boned face had the light tan of early, summer sun.

She was tall, slender and today she'd made a great effort to be fashionable. Her navy blue, silk trouser suit was a good contrast to the blue-and-white striped camisole top she wore underneath. High heels gave her an even more slender elegance and she sat down again to wait, satisfied with her appearance but suddenly feeling a little anxious. Which was strange, because if she didn't get this job, it didn't really matter. Her yearlong spell in a French school had paid well and she wasn't going to starve for six months, whatever Candy and Bob thought.

Her lips tilted in amusement. Six months under Candy's wing – what a thought! She had stayed with Candy and Bob before and it had been harrowing. They tried to treat her like one of their young children, even to the extent of bringing her an unexpected gift when the children had one. The heart was in the right place with her sister and brother-in-law, but a weekend with them was just about all she could cope with. The status of wife and mother reached, Candy was always looking for other good deeds to perform. She normally looked towards Alissa.

'Miss Brent?'

Alissa looked up and found Mrs Dobson, the owner of the agency, waiting for her with the door open. It must be an important client if she was dealing with it herself. She'd been rather snooty at the interview the week before and had narrowly missed a dose of Alissa's sarcastic tongue.

Alissa stood slowly, straightened her jacket and walked forward with the confidence she usually felt, the small attack of nerves quite over. Yes or no, it didn't really matter and intimidation was not on the agenda. She was not begging for a job. This was probably more important to the client than it was to her.

They walked down a short corridor and Alissa was aware that she was being inspected surreptitiously. She didn't mind because she knew she looked fine. Her only problem was trying to curb the tendency to grin about it. She was taller than the woman beside her and had a strong desire to look down and fix the boss-lady with quelling eyes. It reminded her of the man in the restaurant. The desire to grin faded fast. She hoped Candy had gone straight home as promised and not lingered to get another look at the gorgeous man.

'In here, Miss Brent.'

The door was opened for her and Alissa went in first, her face quite composed. Apparently, it was always merely a matter of meeting the client and giving them a chance to sum up the applicant. All the questions had been answered already so there couldn't be much to say.

She knew it was a man with a son and daughter. The only thing she didn't know was why he didn't simply send them to school. It would be much less bother than having a stranger living in his house. She hoped he didn't imagine she was about to become a glorified babysitter.

'Mr Tempest, this is Miss Brent.' Mrs Dobson's voice was slightly tinged with awe and as Alissa turned, she quite understood why. She also knew why Mrs Dobson was dealing with this herself, wealth seemed to emanate from the tall man who stood watching her.

Standing, he looked even more alarming than he had done earlier at the restaurant. His face was still utterly devoid of expression, he was simply looking. The piercing grey eyes flashed over her and then pinned her to the spot like a laboratory specimen.

She need not have worried about Candy. The gorgeous man would be no danger to her sister because he was right here and, for the first time in her life, Alissa felt a wave of something very close to fright.

Live in this man's house? Not likely! Being in the same crowded restaurant had been worrying. Being in the same office was even more alarming and the urge to say, 'No, thank you,' and run out was overwhelming.

'Miss Brent, please sit down.' He said it as if he owned the building and Alissa sank to the nearest seat, carefully looking away from the clear eyes without being too obvious about it. He *might* own the building for all she knew. He might own almost anything. He didn't look as if he required any sort of help at all, certainly not a tutor for his children. He could quite easily buy a whole school and just get rid of the other pupils.

He never offered to shake her hand but simply continued to stand and watch her unwaveringly. Mrs Dobson darted round the desk and tried to look as if she had the whole thing under control but Alissa had the distinct feeling that everything was to be left to this man.

'I've read your application form and your letter.' He walked to the window and stood with his back to it. The action was done with an ease borne of long practice and done to put her at a disadvantage. Now all she could see was his towering height, his powerful outline. It made Alissa feel small and that annoyed her. The desire to stand and square up to him flared inside. 'Is there anything you would like to ask me?'

'Yes. I wondered why you wanted a tutor for your children. Surely it would be much more convenient to place them in school?'

Mrs Dobson made a murmur of panicky protest. This was a good way to lose both a job and a client. Alissa could see her bristling with anxiety but it didn't matter. She *did* want to know why these children were not going to school. The fact that he could now watch her at his leisure while she could not see him was annoying but unimportant. He couldn't stand by the window all the time. Sooner or later he would have to move from there and, in any case, she'd already seen him twice today, both at the restaurant and here.

Seeing him once had been more than enough. This little interview was merely a polite way of getting out of here fast, because she certainly didn't want the job. At the moment, the idea of white slavers seemed to offer a good alternative. This man made her hair feel as if it were standing on end.

'It's imperative that my children stay with me.' He moved and came closer, leaning against the desk and looking down at her. 'I have a boy of eight and a younger daughter, as you already know from my correspondence with the agency. I have to go away and leaving them behind is not an option at all. They come with me. In two days time, I fly out to Antarra and the children will need a tutor while I'm there. They can't miss school for six months.'

Alissa stared right through him, seeing his face but stiffening with suspicion. Antarra? She'd never heard of it. One thing she did know, it was not near England and that would have been quite enough to put her off, even if she hadn't felt this instant rejection of him on sight. This man would be unpredictable in the middle of a busy market. If he *had* been a film star, the other actors would have required danger money to work with him.

She did not blunder into peril – that was Candy's prerogative. Out in some unknown place he would be able to do exactly as he liked and children would be no sort of protection. Oh no! This job was a non-starter.

'I couldn't possibly leave England, Mr Tempest,' she said, allowing her eyes to focus on him again.

He instantly looked exasperated and regarded her with a very black frown. 'You have six months free. You've already been overseas for a year, according to your letter. Why is it impossible to leave again for a short while?'

'Perhaps I phrased it wrongly. It's not impossible.' She forced herself to face him head on and her dark eyes looked right back into his cold, crystal gaze. 'I don't *intend* to leave England. I have my own job back in six months and this is really just a way of filling in time.'

'You don't need the money, Miss Brent?'

'As a matter of fact, I don't.' A little smile edged her lips and he scowled at her fiercely before abandoning the desk and pacing up and down. Mrs Dobson was almost at the stage of putting her head in her hands but all Alissa wanted to do was leave fast.

'I'll double the salary.'

He spun round as he snapped out the words and Mrs Dobson perked up. Double salary meant double fees. Alissa, however, felt a shivering wave of suspicion run completely down her spine.

'I'm sorry.' She stood and collected her bag. 'This has obviously been a waste of your valuable time. I'm sure some other teacher will be found who is suitable.'

'I chose you. You were the best person for the job and I don't have time to start all over again.'

'Then you'll have to put off your departure.' Alissa was greatly irritated by the way he was trying to browbeat her. She nodded pleasantly to Mrs Dobson who just stared back in shock and then she turned to the door.

'Wait!' He spoke imperiously but Alissa barely glanced at him.

'It would be pointless, Mr Tempest. I've taken up enough of your time as it is. Goodbye.' She walked out and closed the door, resisting the urge to run along the short corridor and put at least two buildings between herself and this daunting man. Gorgeous he may be, and at close quarters he looked as handsome as the devil, but he brought out every instinct of self-preservation she possessed. Two buildings distant was not nearly enough. Two counties might just do the trick.

She stepped out on to the pavement feeling as if she had just escaped some major calamity. Thank goodness Candy hadn't been with her. At the moment, Alissa felt as if she had made a daring getaway and didn't need the added chore of looking after Candy. She stepped out with a sigh of relief but it changed to a gasp of shock as a hard hand closed over her arm.

'Just a minute, Miss Brent!'

The frightening man had her in his grasp and Alissa turned with more calm on her face than she felt. She looked up haughtily and met furious eyes.

'I need your assistance,' he snapped, 'and you're coming with me to Antarra if I have to take you by that long hair and drag you there.'

She couldn't pull away but her temper rose rapidly and she glared into his annoyed face.

'I can scream very loudly. If you don't let go of my arm, I intend to start screaming right now.'

For a second he continued to stare at her, then his lips twisted in self-disparagement as his hand fell away. The silver eyes narrowed on her face and she saw a sort of unwilling admiration in the startlingly clear depths.

'Have a coffee with me. I'm not a dangerous lunatic. I really need your help. You're the one for the job and I'm at the stage where I'm willing to beg.'

'That would take a lot of believing.' She had to look up a very long way to meet those compelling eyes and to be towered over was something extremely new to her. It was also annoying.

'I'm in trouble.' He sounded serious but Alissa gave him a very sceptical look.

'Buy your way out of it, Mr Tempest. I'm sure you could.'

'Ordinarily, yes. Some things can't be corrected with money however. At the moment I need distance from here. I need loyalty, I need someone with a cool head and courage. In other words, I need you.'

'You don't know me at all. For all you know I might be timid as a mouse and utterly devious.'

'I'm quite accustomed to summing people up. In my business, I need the ability. You're cool and courageous. If you give your loyalty it will not fail. Two children need you. So do I.'

'You're making things difficult for me, Mr Tempest.'

Alissa looked at him severely. She gave him a few marks for persistence and another few for calling her people and not a woman. It took just a little of the edge off his chauvinistic attitude.

'Damn it, I'm trying to make it difficult!' He stared at her irritably. 'Have a coffee with me and I'll make it more difficult still.'

Alissa's lips twitched in unwilling amusement and she nodded. 'All right, but don't take anything for granted. I'm not easy to fool.'

'That I can well believe.' He gave her an irritated look but he took her arm again politely, abandoning his previous steel-like grasp. 'This way, Miss Brent. I can spare about half an hour to persuade you, after that I must get back to the children.'

'You may not have persuaded me at all.'

'It will rest with your conscience. I realise I can't follow my inclination to drag you away with us and then have the satisfaction later of saying, "I told you so". I'll have to see what you think.'

He was going to use his powers of persuasion at full tilt. Alissa knew that and she imagined his powers of persuasion were very good indeed. She had no intention of going anywhere with him but going for a coffee was better than standing in the street and shouting at each other, and she had not liked the idea of pulling free and taking to her heels either. It would have been the first time in her life she had run away from anything or anyone.

It was also intriguing that he should be prepared to go to all this trouble to hire her. That mystery alone was worth the risk of having a coffee with him. She went along quietly, ignoring him when he glanced sideways at her with obvious exasperation.

To her surprise, he steered her to a rather shabby coffee bar. Alissa would not have dreamed of going in there herself and he looked too expensive for this sort of place. If he wanted a quiet chat then he was in for a disappointment. The whole place would come to a startled standstill.

'This is not my sort of place.' She glanced at him as he opened the door for her.

'I'm glad to hear it. It is, however, the nearest place. I have no time to spare and you are unwilling to give me any time at all. Under the circumstances we'll have to work with the materials to hand. This place is to hand. After you, Miss Brent.'

Alissa gave him a caustic look and entered. Apart from saying, 'Won't' and standing there stubbornly, she had no alternative.

There were plastic tables, hastily wiped over and that done probably because they'd seen him coming. Fortunately, the place was empty. The amazed look they got from the girl behind the counter was enough to make Alissa seethe and her temper didn't improve when he politely held a chair for her. It was plastic too, red and not altogether clean.

'This place is private.'

'This place is outrageous!' she corrected him in a low voice filled with annoyance. 'The girl at the counter will probably pull up a chair and join us. Perhaps you should write down your comments, Mr Tempest, and pass them across to me?'

'Nobody will join us.' He turned and fixed the girl with his rather scary eyes. 'Two coffees please and we're in a hurry.'

The waitress scuttled off and Alissa knew for sure that she would cower in the back until they left. Under the circumstances, she would have done exactly the same thing herself, even though she didn't take kindly to any sign of male dominance.

Alissa glanced at him secretly, reminding herself she didn't know anything about this man. All the same, she realised that inside she was almost bubbling with excitement. This was different. Not like school, nothing humdrum and, cautious though she was, she sensed a feeling of adventure in the air just by being in his presence.

When he looked up and met her assessing gaze, Alissa quickly looked away. If she was to maintain the upper hand it would not do to have him thinking anything about him intrigued her. She already knew that maintaining the upper hand with him was paramount, even if their association was limited to one cup of coffee. There must be no false moves with him or he would pounce. The idea intrigued Alissa even more. She'd been looking for adventure all her life and this was the nearest thing to it.

The coffee was served quickly and the girl disappeared as Alissa expected. He started right away and she steeled herself for an interesting battle. Now they were actually down to the matter, she was not too sure about her decision to come here with him. Shouting in the street would perhaps have been a better idea after all. He had somehow managed to move a step closer. It would have been much easier to have turned and walked off in the street.

'Why did you refuse the job?'

He asked the question abruptly, no finessing around the thought and Alissa decided to finish this at once. No matter how interesting the thought of battle was she would not countenance this.

The curt way he spoke was quite indicative of his attitude. She had refused politely and firmly back there in the office. Now his manner suggested she had been playing some sort of silly, feminine game. His attitude was to get the nonsense over with and settle matters at once – to his own satisfaction.

'I don't like you.' She stated it clearly and calmly, meeting his unwavering stare.

His lips tilted in a way that now bordered on very real amusement. 'You don't throw a small stone when a large rock is available, do you, Miss Brent? I suspect many people dislike me. Yet they work for me all the same.'

'Perhaps they have to, Mr Tempest. I don't.'

'You do. You're exactly what I need – quick, fierce, independent and irritating.'

'Is that supposed to be a compliment…?' Alissa's cheeks flushed as she challenged him angrily.

He gave her a sardonic glance. 'I don't hand out compliments Miss Brent and, if I did, you would merely regard me with greater suspicion. You seem to imagine I have some deadly plan in mind that will lead to your temporary or even permanent disappearance.'

'I merely pointed out that I do not intend to leave England.'

'Don't spare my feelings, Miss Brent, you haven't spared them so far. I realise you would quickly count your fingers if I tried to shake hands with you.'

'Look! Let's get our facts straight shall we? You offered a job. I refused it. This is an astonishing way of doing business. If I applied for a job at a supermarket and then declined the offer, the manager would not rush out after me, drag me to a café and interrogate me about my reasons.'

'I know your reasons, Miss Brent. You dislike me, you're suspicious of me and, oddly enough, you're secretly afraid of me.'

'There's nothing odd about it. Instincts are very good things to follow. My instinct is to steer clear of anyone like you. I even warned my sister not to look at you at the restaurant.'

She stopped abruptly, realising her tongue was slightly out of control but he actually gave a low laugh, the amusement back in his clear eyes.

'I noticed. You made a very good job of it too. She fled rapidly, using you as a shield until she was out in the open air and safe. It gave me a very buoyant feeling of supernatural power. Not everyone recognises me as Dracula.'

'Time's up, Mr Tempest.' Alissa looked at him icily. 'If you spent a whole week at this, you would not persuade me to join you at this mysterious place you're planning to visit.'

She began to stand but his hand came down over hers and his grip was so strong that she sank back to her seat, annoyance in her eyes.

'Three weeks ago,' he said before she could utter any word of protest, 'a car came along the road as my children were walking from the park with their nanny. It stopped and before she could do anything, my son was pulled into the car and the man beside the driver was reaching for my daughter. The nanny screamed and hung on tightly to my little girl and the car left without her. Then a strange thing happened. An unknown woman followed and daringly rescued my son but refused to leave her full name. *You* are that woman, Miss Brent.'

'James is *your* son?' Alissa was too stunned to do more than stare at him in awe. 'How did you find me?'

'I have a lot of people at my disposal. They searched for you. It was also useful that my son took down your car number.'

Alissa felt quite numb. So much for good deeds. She had expected to be offered a diamond necklace. She hadn't reckoned on being forced into his life.

'You had no idea I was about to start looking for a job.'

'Your previous employers had a letter of enquiry from the agency, so it was quite simple really. I would have tried to persuade you to come with me in any case. However, opportunity knocked and at no time do I let Fate get the upper hand.'

They sat staring at each other. Alissa couldn't believe she had been tracked down so effortlessly. Nor could she believe that someone could be so quick to grasp an opportunity.

'Have the police caught the men who tried to kidnap James?' Alissa showed every sign of staying now and the hand over hers was removed.

'No, they haven't. I called them initially and then continued the conversation when James came back home. However, I told them it had all been settled. I'm not too keen on police involvement. I intend to catch these people myself but it's rather more complicated than that. One of the people who tried to take my children was my wife's brother.'

Alissa just looked at him, trying to work all this out. A relative had tried to kidnap his children? That was what he was telling her. His wife's brother. Where was his wife then? She asked him outright.

'What about your wife, Mr Tempest? What does she have to say about all this?'

'My ex-wife to be correct. She probably had something to do with it but I have no proof at the moment. I only have the word of my son that his uncle tried to take him away. The nanny is new and would never have recognised Carl. My son's word, however, is quite good enough for me.'

'They were trying to take the children to their mother,' Alissa surmised slowly and his bitter laugh startled her into looking up at him.

'Most likely. She is now married to a reprobate who can

match her schemes move for move. James would have been out of the country within hours and Sally too, if they'd managed to get her.'

'But if their mother wants to see them…'

'She wants money, Miss Brent. She married into money and cheated her way out of it. Now she wants the money back. She does not want her children. She merely wants them as hostages because she knows I'll do anything to spare them from the knowledge of her faults and anything to keep them from the attentions of the man she married.'

'Their mother? Surely…?' Alissa began and he moved impatiently, glancing at her in frustration.

'All women are not gentle, Miss Brent, just as all men are not villains. Cynthia wants money. That is all she wants, all she has ever wanted. A letter containing details of how I could buy them back would have followed the disappearance of the children.'

'You should let the police deal with everything,' Alissa insisted, quite seeing that he was desperate about this.

'My ex-wife and her swine of a husband live in Europe. I did not want months of investigation while the police forces of several nations attempted to track them down. By the time they were found, James would have been exposed to the character of his mother and her husband for too long. I manage my own affairs. My wife will not get the chance to make a second attempt. But first, I want safety for my children and there is only one place where I can guarantee it – Antarra.'

Alissa watched him carefully, biting at her lower lip and summing things up. She could see he needed help if all this was true. He had obviously had her thoroughly investigated and she could bet he hadn't relied on the agency for that. He was too razor-sharp to leave anything to chance.

She had merely played into his hands when she went to the agency. He had some very good investigators and he looked as if he could afford to surround himself with an army of them. Candy would assume he was a crook, a gangster, and a sinister member of the underworld. She wasn't sure herself.

'How do I know this story is true? How do I know James is your son?'

He watched her with more patience than she had given him credit for. He then took a piece of paper from his inside breast pocket and handed it to her. It was a newspaper cutting, several days old and the headline over the article said, 'Kidnap Attempt on Children of Financier'. There was a photograph of Kieran Tempest and one of his children. In the photograph, James could be nobody else but the son of the man who sat opposite, the likeness was incredible. There was also the photograph of the delightful little girl Alissa had seen before. The words below were all the proof she needed. 'On Friday morning, the children of financier Kieran Tempest were involved in an attempted abduction a few yards from his London home.'

Alissa looked up at him and handed the paper back silently. He took it and just stared at her for a second and then he said quietly, 'I need someone I can trust. I need a good teacher for James but much more than that, I need a woman who will use her eyes and her instincts to help my children at all times. You speak your mind. You've already acted as your instincts dictated. You may not like me but you and I are the same kind of people. Will you come with us, Miss Brent?'

'How did the Press get on to this?'

He shrugged impatiently. 'How do they get on to anything? There's always somebody willing to earn a little more by slipping information to the papers. I made a call, somebody took it. That's all they needed. You can surely see why I want my children out of here?'

Alissa continued to chew at her lip, her eyes meeting his. At the back of those clear eyes she imagined she could see a slight desperation and it was obviously a very new feeling for this powerful man. He was going to hole up somewhere to protect his children. That too would be a new experience for him, because a man like Kieran Tempest would act at once in any situation with no thought of personal danger.

'Please,' he said and Alissa made up her mind.

'All right. I'll go with you. I'll have to make arrangements for my house, my things and...'

'When this is over, I'll buy you a house. I'll buy you anything you like, anything you want. Right now I need to leave and I can't wait until you've packed up this and that, stopped the milk and papers and put the cat into a suitable holiday home.'

'Don't start harassing me, Mr Tempest! No milk, papers or cat. Give me twenty-four hours and I'll be knocking at your door.'

'Very well. Twenty-four hours and not a second more.' He was looking at her intently and Alissa hid a renewed burst of annoyance. She was going to have trouble with this man because she would not stand for any browbeating.

'Any sign of tyranny and I'll leave, wherever we happen to be.' She looked straight into his eyes.

'I will try to curb my desire to beat you from time to time, Miss Brent. I wish you to remain exactly as you are, fierce and irritating. It would not suit my purpose to have you cowed and dominated.'

'I'm glad to hear it because it would be impossible. We can probably come to some amicable arrangement.'

'Amicable? Surely that would be hoping for too much? I'll settle for the ferocity.'

'I am not ferocious. I teach very quiet girls.'

'I can imagine. Discipline will not be a problem with my children, however. Just teach and watch.'

Alissa gathered her bag and stood quickly, looking down her nose at him in a very severe manner before he could get to his feet. 'I must warn you that I am not looking forward to being in your employ, Mr Tempest.'

'But you promised. A woman like you is invariably true to her word.'

'You have a great deal of faith in your own judgement.'

'And in you, Miss Brent. That's why I chose you.' He stood and towered over her. 'Twenty-four hours, to the second.'

Alissa walked out quickly and when she looked back, he was at the door of the coffee bar watching her. Surely he didn't think she was going to be attacked, a fierce person like herself? He was apparently expecting her to take on all-comers, so she was quite capable of getting back to the main road without mishap. Then again, he was probably just standing there to send out last minute vibes of intimidation.

She wondered if she had done the right thing in agreeing to go with him. Probably not, but she was in it now. He was right of course, she had given her word and she would see it through. Besides, the whole thing was scented with adventure. Even now she could feel it swirling around her.

She had taken the job in Europe for some sort of adventure, although none had been forthcoming. This was very different, like the plot from a book. And then, of course, there were the children who obviously needed someone. She was quite capable of facing the music no matter what the tune. She was not at all like Candy. That last thought brought a grimace to her face. Her sister would have to be told.

'You are out of your stubborn mind!' Candy raged when the whole thing had been explained to her. 'It gave me enough worry when you went off to Europe by yourself, but this is too much Alissa.'

'Somebody has to help those children and don't say you still think it's a trick. I rescued James. I was actually there. I saw the newspaper cutting with his photograph and Kieran Tempest's photograph beside it.'

'And how very strange for him to be carrying the news-paper cutting round with him,' Candy shot back. 'Surely you realise that, Alissa? He was all prepared for setting you up.'

'There's no doubt at all about who he is,' Bob Greaves said, coming into the room and draping his arm around his wife's shoulders. 'The City calls him "Mr Money".'

'There are villains in the City as elsewhere,' Candy pointed out, shrugging angrily to free herself. 'The fact is, Alissa is sorry for him.'

'I don't even like him!'

'Instinct,' Candy said with a look of triumph. 'Who was it not too long ago who pointed out her own unassailable instincts? Tell me that.'

'This is different. I'm thinking of the children.'

'You're a soft touch.'

'I am hard as nails and extremely level-headed. This is a well-paid position to last until I'm back with my own girls.'

'Who may not see you again if you sail off to this Antarra place with that pirate.'

'Candy! I've had enough. I'm going and I don't want to hear another word about it,' Alissa glared at her sister.

'Let's face it, Alissa,' Bob interrupted. 'This is all because you want adventure.'

'Keep out of this, Bob,' his wife snapped. 'Alissa is my sister.'

'And my sister-in-law, but I wouldn't dream of getting between you two when you're fighting.'

'We are not fighting,' Alissa said with a calmness she no longer felt. 'I'm going now in any case. I have a lot of packing to do.'

She kissed Candy who was now crying, her measure of last resort that Alissa was adept at ignoring. Bob gave her a grin and a hug and Alissa kissed the children.

'I'll be back soon,' she promised.

'Are you a soft touch, Aunt Alissa?' The shaking voice of Candy's oldest daughter gave Alissa a twinge as nothing else had.

'Certainly not, Ginny. I'm a vicious, frightening sort of person. I have sharp horns under my hair.'

Alissa made her escape, leaving Ginny giggling and Bob supporting a weeping Candy who would dry her tears the moment Alissa's car was out of sight. It was all par for the course. The same scene had happened when Alissa had ventured to Europe.

This was not quite the same however. This time she might well be in someone's power and unable to retreat.

'Rubbish!' Alissa said it loudly and felt a whole lot better. Kieran Tempest was well known, a respected businessman. She had seen the children and had even rescued James. What could possibly go wrong? She was about to have an adventure. She would live in luxury, if his appearance was anything to go by, and he'd offered double the salary. What more could she want?

Alissa ignored the soft voice of warning that whispered up her spine. She burst loudly into song to keep the soft warning quiet and drove along to pack her belongings.

chapter three

Forty-eight hours later, Alissa sat in a private jet that was taking her to Antarra. It had all happened so swiftly that, even now, she could scarcely believe it. Only the sight of the handsome, cold-faced man who sat across the aisle from her assured her it was true, that and the little boy who sat next to his father with his eyes firmly closed in an attempt to sleep.

James had the same black hair, the same striking features as his father and Alissa's eyes moved to the fair head that rested on her lap. Sally was very different, angelic, a picturebook child who was sunny and bright and she had made her mind up to love Alissa on sight. Sitting by Alissa and using her lap as a cushion had been her own idea entirely.

Alissa rested her head back and tried to sleep. It was not easy. From the moment she had presented herself at the splendid London home of Kieran Tempest, she had seemed to slip almost casually into his well-organised life. Her car had been driven away and locked in some large garage. She had been shown to a room whose luxury had overwhelmed her.

Apart from meeting her in the gleaming hall, looking at her intently and giving a satisfied nod of approval at her punctuality, she hadn't seen him at all. He hadn't dined with her. She had eaten in solitary splendour and found herself very edgy in case he suddenly appeared.

He did not, however, and the last words he had spoken had been to tell her rather curtly that they would leave at first light. They had, and now she was here without any real idea of where they were heading. All she knew was the name Antarra.

Too many ideas were running through her mind now to allow for peaceful sleep. There were too many questions and it was impossible to say with any real truth that her suspicions about Kieran Tempest had been completely cast off.

The biggest of these was about his wife. What sort of woman would try to involve her own children in a plot to force money from the man she had once married? The only woman Alissa really knew with children was Candy, and Candy would fight tooth and nail to protect her children from any danger. Candy even tried to protect her, even though she was totally incapable of the feat. What sort of world did these people live in? Was their behaviour really governed by great wealth?

Alissa opened her eyes and looked carefully across at the man who was occupying her thoughts to the exclusion of anything else. There was no doubting his wealth. She had done some investigating herself in the short time after she had agreed to go with him. What Bob had said was true. Kieran Tempest *was* money, a financier, wealthy beyond most people's wildest imaginings.

In the physical sense, he owned nothing at all, except for a house in London and another in Italy. He didn't own a factory or anything to produce goods or even sell them. What he did own was money, and he apparently moved it about astutely in the money markets, making more money all the time.

An article she had read had been most informative. Apparently, those with big money watched Kieran Tempest to see where his money would go next, knowing that to catch a ride on the tails of his brilliant reasoning would make them millions. Unfortunately, they were more often than not too late. He had a feel for things that others did not possess to quite the same degree.

She wondered just how ruthless he was. She wondered how often that clever brain rested. Even now, he was working, a great sheaf of papers lying on the hard briefcase on his lap. Alissa tried to see without moving her head forward. There was hardly any writing, the papers contained just a great mass of figures. It was alarming. It was a wonder he didn't speak in some sort of mathematical code. But there again, he had worked out exactly whom he wanted with him in some relentless, mathematical way. He needed her and so she would have to be available.

Even his hands suited the picture. She had already felt the strength of his touch and now they moved swiftly over the page with long-fingered accuracy, graceful in a way – strong and graceful – very masculine. So was a male tiger. Both were dangerous too. She should not let that fact slip from her mind.

Not that she would. It was the children who had touched her heart and his obvious sincerity when he spoke of them. There wasn't much doubt about his paternal love and he seemed to get on with them very well. There was the adventure though, the thought of that brightened her.

'Try to sleep, Miss Brent. We still have a long flight in front of us.'

Alissa looked up from her intense contemplation of his hands to find him watching her. 'What time do we land?'

He glanced at the slim, gold watch on his wrist. 'Five hours from now. We then have another journey. It would be wise to rest while you can. Sally seems to be determined to stay with you. She may be equally determined that you carry her.' He glanced down at the beautiful child who slept quietly with her head on Alissa's lap and when he looked up again, his eyes were narrowed and watchful. 'I'm placing a great deal of reliance on you, Miss Brent. I have to make snap judgements in almost everything I do but I've never made a judgement that means so much to me.'

Alissa felt the shiver race down her spine again. She had come headlong into this situation with her eyes wide open, all because of the children and her pity for this powerful man. If anything went wrong he would probably kill her without thinking twice about it.

'I had to make a quick decision too, Mr Tempest. I could simply have waited for my old job to resurface or I could have stayed with my sister and her husband.'

'Why didn't you stay with them?'

'They suffocate me. Candy would like to feed me with a spoon and Bob is always looking for potential rapists.' She shrugged her slim shoulders. 'To become involved in a thickening plot seemed to me to be much the safer bet.'

Kieran's lips curved in an unexpectedly genuine smile. It did miracles for his face and his eyes looked less alarming too, warm for a minute.

'I'll try to see to it that the plot does not touch you in any way. You are my unexpected surprise, the card up my sleeve but if it ever comes to that, we'll be in difficulties.'

'I *had* worked that out for myself. However, if it comes to it, I've got a very bad temper.' She looked up. 'I like to win, Mr Tempest, whatever I'm doing. I'll not just close my eyes and hope to die.'

'I know, that's why you're here. I rely on your prying, suspicious mind too.' His lips turned down sceptically when she looked at him with a feigned, innocent annoyance. 'I'm well aware that your steady contemplation of me just now was one of distrust. Keep it up. It may serve us both very well. Do not, however, look for chinks in my armour. I closed them long ago.'

He went back to his papers and Alissa noticed the hardness of his face seemed even more pronounced. She could guess why he had closed all chinks in his armour. His wife must have been a terrible woman – if it were all true.

She could not find out more at the moment and Alissa tried to sleep, her hand resting for a second on the gleaming fair head close to her. Whatever was going on, nobody would get the chance to hurt the children. Her lips set as firmly as his. She was here to help the children and she would help them – at any cost.

They had been flying through the night and as Alissa awoke later, they were just beginning to descend. A glance at Kieran Tempest assured her that he was wide-awake and looking as alert as usual. There was no sign of tiredness on his face and after quickly checking the children, Alissa peered out of the small window beside her.

The plane was over the sea, losing height rapidly. The sun was just rising, its brilliant light sending the night-clouds fleeing before it, making the sky a picture of red, turquoise and burning gold which reflected in a dark sea. The whole place breathed tropics at her and Kieran Tempest had warned her to bring clothes for hot weather. But in spite of her frantic, last minute investigations, Alissa had not discovered the exact location of Antarra.

Antarra had proved to be a place of mystery because it was not on any map she had been able to consult. The geography teacher at her old school hadn't heard of it either. The children should be fairly safe in this lost place, unless the enemy already knew all about Antarra, unless Kieran Tempest had brought his wife there in the past.

Alissa frowned and rested back in her seat. She must keep a close watch on her loyalties. She was already classing the ex-wife and uncle as the enemy. Which was all very well, providing her taciturn employer had told the complete truth. His ex-wife worried her most. After his story at the coffee bar, Alissa had looked upon the children's mother as some sort of wicked, black-clad witch, but she still could not quite make herself believe that a woman existed who had no feelings at all for her own children. Something felt wrong and until she found out the whole truth, she would have to play this carefully.

Sally stirred and Alissa took her to the small, neat washroom. As they came back, coffee was being served with fruit juice for the children. Sally settled down happily by Alissa, not one bit fretful after her time of rather uncomfortable sleep. This morning however, James looked as forbidding as his father and he drank his juice steadily. He didn't even glance across at Alissa and his small sister.

'We've arrived then?' Alissa ventured as the plane touched down at a small, still-dark airport. The sun was only just beginning to hit the runway, the brilliant light they had seen higher up not yet visible here.

'By no means,' Kieran said. 'We go on to Antarra tomorrow. There are things here we may need and during the day I'll get them, because once at our destination, we will not be making many expeditions into civilisation. We also need a little real sleep and I have to alert certain people to the fact that we're almost there.'

Alissa nodded and said nothing but as she collected her things and helped Sally out of her seat, her lips were tightly compressed. This might just be the biggest mistake of her life. One thing she now knew, they were not to be in contact with other people or, at least, nobody he considered to be part of civilisation.

The little hand that clutched hers as they left the plane was a great source of comfort. James looked about as comforting as his father. He had glanced at her with dark, unreadable eyes and then looked away. All he had ever been since she had met him was scrupulously polite, Alissa's advances being met with a very firm, 'No thank you,' whatever she was suggesting at the time.

Kieran stepped on to the tarmac, stopped and held up his arms to lift Sally down. Before Alissa could gather her wits, he had offered the same courtesy to her. It was only a small jump down and James had managed it easily. Alissa had expected to do the same thing but two strong hands spanned her waist and held there.

He looked up, meeting her eyes before lifting her down with a great deal of care. For a second, Alissa felt she was floating on air, then she was standing, slightly breathlessly, beside her little party, a cool breeze blowing from the sea fanning her hot face.

Alissa felt flustered but he just turned away, scooped Sally up into his arms and led the way across to the low, white buildings that were now beginning to catch the rays of the rising sun. Alissa followed quickly. She did not wish to be left behind by even one foot but she felt decidedly wobbly inside after the brief, physical contact with Kieran.

He scared her. She admitted it. Her instincts when she had first seen him had not played her false. She had allowed herself to be persuaded into a situation that was nothing at all to do with her and she bit her lip worriedly. How long would this go on?

Perhaps he wouldn't need her for the entire six months? He lived in a world unlike hers, a world of power, wealth and, apparently, danger. What would his reaction be if she suddenly announced she wished to leave? Ferocious probably. More ferocity than she could ever hope to summon up in spite of his peculiar belief in her untamed character.

Maybe things would be a little more relaxed on Antarra because Kieran was about as relaxed as a large hunting cat and James was little better. Getting close to James would be a problem. She could imagine he would do his lessons stonily and probably brilliantly. He might also speak only when spoken to.

At the moment, this small family would quite likely take all her capabilities without having to keep alert for outside danger. She hoped the tall, dark man in front of her still intended to double her salary.

'I've booked us into here,' Kieran said, opening a door for Alissa as they walked along the passage of the small hotel close to the airfield. 'Keep Sally with you. I'll take James.'

It was all obviously well planned. The room had twin beds and as their hand luggage was brought, Alissa gazed longingly at the soft-looking bed she would sleep on. She had vowed not to be a glorified nanny but it seemed Sally had decided otherwise.

'Can I go to sleep now, Lissa?'

Alissa cast aside her own tiredness to take control. 'Right now, we'll give you a quick bath and then it's off to bed until much, much later.' She kicked off her own shoes and went forward to see to the tired little girl.

When she looked up, Kieran was still standing in the doorway, his jaw tensed. There was a look in his eyes that threatened violence to anyone who tried to harm this child and Alissa suddenly felt a wave of unexpected sympathy for him.

'I'll sleep with one eye open,' she promised and he made a very obvious attempt to relax. His mouth twisted ruefully at his own anxiety and he nodded, turned to the door and left.

Alissa cleaned her face and almost fell into bed. Sally was already deeply asleep and as far as Alissa could see they were safe for the time being. It would not be necessary to sleep with one eye open because she was quite sure that in the adjoining room, Kieran was already doing that.

Maybe he didn't need to sleep, she thought tiredly. Maybe he was devoid of all human emotion? Her eyes closed on this rather intriguing thought and she drifted towards a troubled sleep with a dark, harshly handsome face swimming before her closed eyelids.

Being sympathetic to a man like Kieran Tempest was nothing short of idiotic. Sympathy made one vulnerable, which was all very well, providing the object of the sympathy was equally vulnerable. Unfortunately, Kieran Tempest was not. He would fight his way out of anything and take the children along under his arm.

What about her? She had the feeling she would be ploughed underfoot if all that power was given free rein. She was probably going to need all the sympathy she could muster, for use on her own behalf.

Alissa muttered irritably and turned firmly on her side. Idle speculation, panic-driven reactions. Pointless. She would play things as they came and, after all, it was just possible that nothing would happen anyway. They were going into hiding, but a hiding place was useless if the other side knew about it. Whatever else Kieran Tempest was, he was certainly not stupid. Things would be all right – at double the salary.

She fell asleep working out how much she would make over a period of three months. He would not need her for longer. In fact, he would probably need her for far less time than that. As soon as his children were safely tucked up, he would take any ruthless sort of action he thought necessary. If his ex-wife had any sense she would be hiding too. It was a bit like waking an immortal. Nothing would stop him.

Cynthia, whoever she was and wherever she was, had made a *very* bad mistake. Having been married to Kieran Tempest she clearly should have known better.

The next day she awoke to find Kieran standing in her room watching her and Alissa's instantaneous feeling of guilt, for having the temerity to sleep at all, was swiftly overtaken by one of outrage that he had invaded her privacy.

'What do you want?' She sat up in bed, pulling the sheet around her and stared at him indignantly.

'I came to tell you that we leave in exactly one hour. Breakfast will be served in your room and the children will eat with you. I have a few things to see to before we go.'

Apparently that was all, and Alissa had been instantly dismissed from his mind, relegated to the position of child-minder. It was obvious too why he was having breakfast served here. She was not to mix with anyone – whoever they might be.

'Just one moment!' A glance at the other bed had assured her that Sally was still deeply asleep so there was no need for diplomacy. 'From this point on, I need more information.'

'For what reason?' He turned and gave her a suspicious glance. 'You know this has been a stopover on our way to Antarra. We arrive there today. You have all the other necessary information.'

'I have no idea where we are. For all I know, Antarra is a mythological location you invented yourself. As to *this* place, I've seen a darkened airfield and one bedroom situated on a dimly-lit corridor.'

'Then I suggest you get up and open the curtains, Miss Brent. You are not in a time capsule. As to Antarra, you'll see it when we arrive.'

'If we arrive!' Alissa glared at him.

His dark brows rose in arrogant surprise. 'I'm trying to prevent a further kidnapping attempt. I really do not have the time, or the inclination, to perpetrate one myself. There is this theory that kidnappers become fascinated by their captives. I chose you for the attributes of your character. You are clever, fierce, irritating and suspicious. Given a choice, I like gentle women.'

Alissa gave a shout of laughter, clapping her hand over her mouth to suppress more of the same. *Gentle*! He would crush anyone gentle to a fine powder.

He glared at her. 'We leave in one hour, Miss Brent. I suggest you wake Sally and get ready yourself. James will be here in a few moments.'

He left and Alissa hurried to the bathroom, seething with a mixture of amusement and indignation, frowning at her own face in the mirror and wondering how she had managed to walk right into giving him a splendid opportunity to insult her. Now he probably expected her to be feeling extremely childish and way below her station in life.

And who would appeal to a man like that? Gentle was out of the question. He would despise anyone who was gentle, that had merely been a put-down for her. She could not even begin to imagine the sort of woman he would find suitable. The fact that he had ever been married at all was astonishing. He was a cold-blooded calculating machine, quite probably immortal as she had mused last night. He might just be a well-put-together mechanical device, beautifully made, performance perfect. He certainly didn't sleep and he looked this morning as alert and watchful as he had done last night.

One hour later, she found herself hurrying down the corridor behind Kieran, her irritation in no way lessened. James was walking firmly beside his father and Sally clutched Alissa's hand as she skipped along quite happily.

Bringing up the rear was a porter who carried the overnight bags they had brought from the plane. The rest of the luggage would undoubtedly follow.

Alissa felt definitely jaded. She was hot and Sally looked hot too. She was going to have trouble with James. James had the superior air about him that his father wore like a well-fitting garment. He clearly looked on her female status with disapproval – his father's son. She gave Sally's hand a warm squeeze and was rewarded with a sunny smile. This was her small ally. Kieran was beginning to make her feel quite unsure of herself and that was a new and unwelcome feeling.

A car was waiting for them, driven by a hefty-looking man whose appearance filled Alissa with suspicion. Kieran had conjured him up from somewhere and while she sat in the back with the children, Kieran sat with the driver.

They conversed in low tones. It was a curiously monosyllabic conversation that was just below her level of hearing. Whatever they were saying, however, it was very serious and her heart skipped a beat when she realised they were not going to the airfield at all. They were heading for the sea.

She could see the water glittering ahead of her, the brilliant sunlight on the smooth, rippling surface dazzling her eyes. It was infuriating to realise that she didn't even know what sea it was – and her luggage was on the plane!

'My things!'

She leaned forward and spoke loudly, realising there was the slight edge of panic to her voice and he took his time in replying. He turned very slowly in his seat and aimed another of those amused, scathing looks at her.

'All taken care of, Miss Brent. They were transferred to the boat this morning before you were even awake. We did not leave your clothes behind. The children need a change to more appropriate clothing too.'

He turned away and Alissa flatly refused to look amazed and ask, 'What boat?' There had been a hint of reprimand in his voice and once again she felt like an inadequate child-minder. She was not accustomed to planning what clothes a child would wear next morning. Her girls at school arrived smart and clean without any assistance from her.

As far as she was concerned, it had been his duty to point out they would need more than their sleeping gear when they left the plane. It was because of him that Sally looked pinkly uncomfortable, as uncomfortable as she felt herself.

She pulled herself up sharply from her mutinous musings. Kieran Tempest clearly adored his children. He had probably credited her with more sense than she possessed. It had been her own duty to see to the children's needs because, like it or not, she was to be part-teacher, part- childminder and part-bodyguard. Battling with her uncompromising boss was not a good way to begin. She took off her own jacket and opened Sally's dress at the neck before settling back with a resigned sigh.

'When we get on the boat you can put your shorts on,' Kieran promised, turning to smile at his daughter. 'You'll be cool then. Miss Brent can also change her clothes.'

To Alissa's surprise, his eyes were dancing with laughter. Her heated face went warmer and, she was sure, even darker pink when Sally issued forth with, 'Lissa will look nice in a swimsuit. She's beautiful.'

'Of course,' Kieran agreed, one black brow raised as his glance flared over Alissa. 'That's why we brought her with us.'

He turned away and Alissa was left to fume quietly. She had the nasty feeling that the driver was smirking in a surrep-titious manner and she wondered where her good sense and worldly wisdom had gone. Somehow or other, she had been cut down to size since she had met Kieran Tempest and the time with him had only just begun.

There was a big, powerful-looking launch at the jetty, the sort of sleek, expensive craft Alissa had seen in the south of France. Only then she had never dreamed she would be going on such a boat herself. This was quite clearly to be their next form of transport and the man waiting for them looked totally different from the driver of the car. He was tall and slim, a thinker, not a muscle man in any way, and he turned intelligent eyes on Alissa as she came forward with the others.

'Shall I take you out there?' He looked at Kieran but the idea was dismissed instantly.

'No, I'll keep the boat. We don't want to be cut off and I need you elsewhere. You keep the car and get started straight away. I want this settled as soon as possible. Keep me informed – hourly if necessary.'

He didn't bother with introductions and before she could do any serious thinking about the conversation, Alissa found herself being helped on to the boat that rocked slightly with the tide. Kieran didn't even look at his men any more.

'You'll find all you need below deck,' Kieran told her and as she ushered Sally down to the cabin, the boat pulled away with a throaty roar and headed out of the small harbour for the open sea. Wherever Antarra was, she was on her way there, and Alissa felt a sudden wave of excitement that wiped out all her irritation.

It was an adventure after all. This was something she would never forget. Kieran might be cold and exasperating but in the normal course of events she wouldn't have met a man like him. To be spun into his world of power for a while was really quite fascinating and she was as anxious as Sally to be out on the deck, watching the vast expanse of sea.

Before long it became abundantly clear that the children

were well used to being on a boat. They did not have to be cautioned at all. Sally was quite content to sit by Alissa and look at the ever-changing sea. As to James, now in shorts and T-shirt, he stayed by his father and was even allowed to take the wheel from time to time. A competent, self-assured child.

A lot of the tension seemed to have drained from Kieran and when later he signalled Alissa to stand beside him, she had no hesitation in obeying. Making her way carefully forward with Sally's hand safely clasped in hers, Alissa stood beside the wheel and looked across the sea as Kieran pointed.

'Our destination, Miss Brent,' he informed her quietly, 'Antarra.'

An island, rising out of the sea, as yet some distance away but drawing closer by the second, was too far away to show any detail. All she could see was the rugged outline and from this distance she had no idea of its real size. It was hazy, with no sign yet of colour but its shape was unmistakable. There was some sort of mountain set slightly off-centre and it was no ordinary mountain.

'A volcano.' Alissa said it almost to herself and there must have been some sort of awe in her voice because he turned his head to glance at her.

'Just the one.' He sounded amused and Alissa tried to look extremely composed.

'Extinct, of course,' she murmured and he shrugged broad shoulders, dismissing it.

'Dormant. The last time it erupted was in the seventeenth century. From time to time it stirs but there's nothing to worry about. Antarra is quite busy, a thriving place. The people there would not be so happily complacent if there was danger.'

'I'm not afraid, I was simply confused. I didn't know that out here...' Alissa stopped and bit at her lip in vexation. 'Of course, I don't really know where we are so there's little point in speculation.'

To her surprise he gave a sudden low laugh and his hand came to her shoulder.

'Look into the distance, beyond Antarra. You see the darker edge to the horizon? That is not cloud. That's South America. Antarra is an island off the coast. Last night, you slept on a different island. Antarra has no airfield. The people say that in the past when the world was new, one of the volcanoes escaped from the mainland and made it's home on Antarra. It brought good fortune with it. They're quite fond of their volcano. Don't let it worry you.'

'You could have let me know where we were,' Alissa grumbled quietly, a little anxious about his hard, warm hand on her shoulder.

'I imagined you were afraid of nothing, Miss Brent.' His hands went back to the wheel and his voice hardened to normality. 'In any case, I have no inclination to trust people, especially not now.'

'Then why insist that I come here?' Alissa hissed, keeping her voice low. This was a private battle and not one she would normally have engaged in with children present.

'I thought you were fearless.' It was said in an equally low tone, a goading tone, and Alissa had great difficulty in not raising her own voice to a shout.

'I'm not afraid of you or anyone else. I do not feel capable, however, of tackling a volcano head-on. Perhaps when I'm older and more experienced.' She turned away and took Sally with her. 'Let's gather our things. I wouldn't like us to be left without clothes when we get off this boat.'

When she glanced round to glare at him, Kieran was watching the approaching island but he had a grin on his face that warned her he was not above goading her to the limit, in spite of his lofty manner. She went quite huffily to the cabin and spent the time reorganising the luggage until her temper had settled.

Alissa stayed there, keeping Sally happily busy until the sound of engines being cut back and the boat slowing drew her out on to the deck. The time had seemed so short but she had under-estimated the speed of the sleek craft because the sight that met her eyes brought a sharp gasp to Alissa's lips.

Antarra seemed to tower over them like an awesome relic left from the past. It looked almost Jurassic, a place to house giant predators. It loomed straight from the sea, green and tranquil-looking but with such a height to it that Alissa felt nothing but awe as she watched.

They were coasting into a small and obviously private quay. Everything around it was lush, green, with trees coming almost to the sea in places. Pale sands stretched in the sun for as far as she could see, with palm trees bending in their graceful way here and there. It was like a paradise island but at the moment the unexpected sight of it filled Alissa with anxiety.

The volcano now seemed to be closer and higher, although she could tell that it was in fact some distance away. Alissa looked at it with respect. It was not a thing to be either ignored or glossed over despite its sides being richly green with forest. She hoped it was benign. It was certainly quite beautiful.

'The house! The house!' Sally shouted excitedly and even James was smiling broadly. Alissa could understand why. As they coasted into the landing stage, she was able to see a house set well back from the sea, paths leading down to the beach.

If she had been expecting some white, tropical house she would have been disappointed, because this house was stone-built – massive by the look of it – with an old-world grandeur that astonished her. It had wrought iron balconies and many windows with the shutters fastened back. It did not look like an island house.

'Built by the Spaniards.' Kieran glanced at her as she stood gazing up at the house across the wide lawns that spread out in front of it. 'The town is the same, Old Spain. They carried their culture with them.'

'There are ghosts in the house.' James said this with a sly little glance in her direction. 'Men in steel helmets with swords.'

'Good! I'm writing a book about ghosts. You can stay up some nights and watch with me. I've got a camera. You can take the shots.'

The superior little smile died from his face.

Sally giggled. 'Can I come too?'

Alissa smiled down at her. 'Not until you've grown a bit. Things like ghosts are for oldies like James and me. You can wait in bed. But really, I think James is teasing me.'

Teasing was not quite the word she would normally have chosen and, once again, Alissa wondered if there would be trouble with the handsome child who stood ramrod straight by his father and then walked stiffly away to the opposite end of the boat. James had no intention of being anything other than awkward.

Kieran glanced at his son's stiff back. 'You may have trouble there.'

'Not for long. Leave him to me.'

'He has good reasons. I'm sorry. I really thought he would take to you, especially as you rescued him. You're so different from…'

'I'll cope,' Alissa said.

She didn't want to hear whom she was different from and

she did not want to know anything else about Kieran's ex-wife. Whatever Cynthia had done was nothing to her. All she had to do was protect the children and, far from annoying her, James had quite touched her heart with his small attempt to scare her.

If he was hurting inside, she would have to cope with that too. She had taken on this job knowing perfectly well that nothing would be easy, knowing it might well be dangerous. Even now she was not quite sure how she had allowed herself to be talked into it.

But here she was and there was nothing to do but get on with the job. The little hand that clutched at her skirt made up for anything disagreeable – and, of course, there was the double salary.

As for Kieran, she would ignore him. The house looked big enough for that to be possible. Ignoring her employer was not an idea to recommend itself to the wise but she had the feeling that if they were thrown into each other's company too much, they may end up beating each other with the nearest available heavy object.

Why he should have chosen her seemed more surprising by the minute. He would have been far more satisfied with a weak, docile teacher for the children. Someone with a downtrodden character who wouldn't say 'boo' to a goose. For once in his autocratic life, he seemed to have made the wrong choice.

chapter four

As they walked up to the house, the children ran on ahead and Alissa had the feeling she should be running with them, looking for danger. Kieran had made her so edgy and nervous about exposure to a threat that she almost felt they should be walking with weapons drawn and eyes on the bushes.

She felt rather like a new and inadequate member of the Secret Service ordered to guard the President's family.

She was also untrained for the job. She reminded herself that she was merely a teacher but all the same, she was alert because she couldn't help it. Her eyes scanned every possible hiding-place for intruders and lingered on every shadow. She wanted to crouch and peer into bushes, looking in all places at once.

Naturally, she tripped.

Kieran caught her with a timely hand at her elbow and it didn't help when he regarded her with the sort of glance he would give to someone with a loose tile in the upper storeys. His lips quirked too, but he controlled himself and ignored her antics.

'Someone will be down from the house to collect the luggage. The two people who run the house flew from London before us.' He said it as if he was carefully changing the subject to take her mind off her duties as a bodyguard and to keep himself from laughing, but Alissa was too suspicious to be side-tracked.

'But if they came from London how do you know…'

'They've worked for me for many years and their allegiance was certainly not with my wife. Nobody knows where we are and Cynthia doesn't even know Antarra exists.'

'Are you certain about that?'

'Perfectly certain.' He gave her another look as if he doubted her sanity and proceeded firmly towards the house.

All the same, Alissa stayed wary. Kieran was well known, carefully watched, and it seemed to her that wherever he went, people would be marking his progress. For all she knew, their trail to Antarra could be as easy to follow as a path made by rampaging elephants through a cornfield.

This was not some deserted island. People lived here. Besides, the woman at the agency knew because he'd mentioned Antarra in front of her. For that matter, Candy and Bob knew. Who else knew? It seemed to Alissa that he'd left far too many tracks when he made the escape plans. What about all the people who worked for him? They might have mentioned it quite unwittingly.

The two people who met them at the door soon took her attention.

'Mr and Mrs Gregson.' Kieran presented her to the middle-aged couple who greeted them with smiles. 'They came on ahead to prepare things. Miss Brent will be looking after Sally and teaching James. Perhaps you could get her settled comfortably, Martha, while George brings in the luggage?'

The children ran back out into the garden and as Alissa ignored Martha Gregson and turned to go after them, Kieran's hand on her arm stopped her.

'I'll keep an eye on the children. You were not intended to be any sort of nanny.' He suddenly gave a slight smile. 'It's just unfortunate that Sally decided to adopt you. I don't suppose you're used to dealing with small, clinging girls.'

'She's delightful,' Alissa said as her eyes followed the

children. 'Any woman would be overjoyed to have Sally around. I suppose it's natural.'

'The mothering instinct? Not really, Miss Brent. I failed to notice it in Cynthia. Perhaps you're more warm and vulnerable than you care to think?'

'Only with children.'

'The children are the only ones who need your warmth.' He stared at her before turning away. 'Get yourself settled and then look round the house. You have to decide where you want to deal with lessons. No duties until tomorrow. The children will want to explore all over again and in any case, they're too tired to be reasonable.'

He was very aloof again but Alissa ignored his attitude. 'I'll keep Sally suitably occupied at the same time. If she's going to be wandering around while I teach James, I'll be worried. I'd rather have her with me.'

He turned to look at her and then nodded. 'Thank you. Anything you want, just let me know.' He walked out into the garden and Alissa stopped worrying. Kieran was on guard and who would try to come here anyway? He probably had all emergencies covered. Apart from someone wheedling the information from Mrs Dobson at the agency, the only real danger was that his wife might know of the existence of the place. She didn't.

Alissa felt a twinge of conscience at the thought. The woman was their mother and she only had Kieran's word for it that Cynthia was to blame for the kidnap attempt. Perhaps it was someone else? He must have enemies. Anyone with so much wealth had enemies.

James was a troubled child. How could she act wisely when she only had the bare bones of the story? She had done something she hadn't done before in her life; met a man and taken his word for everything. His dark good looks and steely eyes had scared her on sight but here she was, all the same. Even Candy wouldn't have behaved so rashly.

She allowed Martha to shepherd her onwards. Her bedroom was beautiful – the carpet was deep and soft, pale rose and feminine. The room was partly panelled in pale wood, which had the effect of adding a feeling of light and airiness to the large space. The covers on the bed were a soft rose-colour that blended with the carpet, and she had her own balcony that gave a view of the sea. She also had her own bathroom.

Everything was luxurious and after her clothes were unpacked and her toiletries arranged on the shelves in the bathroom, Alissa roamed around the house getting her bearings and trying to decide where she would set up some sort of schoolroom for James. His books and plenty of equipment had been brought with them and Alissa was quite sure she could invent plenty of things to occupy and teach a small girl like Sally.

Looking round the house, Alissa felt quite overawed when she was faced with the grandeur of Old Spain. Kieran had left things as he had found them here, except for the modernising touches to the bedrooms and the kitchen. Alissa silently applauded his taste.

Later, glancing from the window of her room, she saw Kieran in the garden with the two children. He was talking to the gardener but, once again, as with the man who had driven them to the boat, there was more the look of body-guard than gardener to this man. There was no sign of any help other than the people he had brought from London and she was sure that this burly looking gardener had come with the Gregsons.

As another man strolled up and joined in the discussion, Alissa knew they were all under guard. Kieran was clearly taking no chances and trusted nobody. She was beginning to wonder how far he would trust her. She didn't know one more thing about him than she had before and she couldn't quite understand how, from time to time, she felt this odd burst of sympathy.

There was no mistaking his deep affection for the children. It proved that there must be a real person under that hard shell. Of course, there had been a couple of occasions when he had smiled but he was normally far too intelligent and self-assured to be anything but cold and arrogant.

Lunch was served in the garden and Alissa was heartily glad about that. Since their first meeting, there had been no need to sit opposite Kieran and to have his attention focused on her. It was something she could well do without and, at least in the garden, she could look around at the scenery. And it was breathtaking.

The turquoise sea seemed to stretch out to infinity with not another island in sight. The garden, green and well tended, led to the white sands where the sea whispered softly as it crept in with the tide. The sun shone brightly, the breeze blew softly, and Antarra was a piece of paradise set like a jewel in a calm sea.

It was only as dinnertime came around that she found herself with no alternative but to face Kieran. The children were in bed and Alissa had helped Martha to settle them. Now, in a cream, silky top that came to her hips and a long pleated skirt to match, Alissa went down to the old, arched dining-room with more misgivings inside than she had ever felt in her life.

Kieran's eyes flicked over her when she came into the room but his expression gave nothing away. He simply stared at her, making her feel very uncomfortable. There was a huge dining table that was in itself intimidating because, although there were only the two of them, Martha had set things extremely formally with Alissa was at one end and Kieran at the other.

The furniture was the heavy, carved oak that seemed to be of original Spanish design. The room appeared to soar above them with curved beams that were dark and hung with huge chandeliers. There was a long, ornate sideboard, weighed down with silver and as to the chairs, Alissa thought they were the nearest things to thrones she had ever seen.

Her eyes darted round the overwhelming room while Kieran sat in his silence and in spite of her normal rebellious state of mind, Alissa found it hard to face him with any show of composure. With this man, it was either fight or hide. She wasn't much given to hiding.

When he suddenly stood and moved her place setting closer to him, she wasn't too sure about the hiding bit.

'You're a very unusual sort of teacher,' he said when she still went on staring around the room and avoiding his eyes.

Alissa looked at him quickly and then looked away. 'Like everyone else, teachers vary.'

'Perhaps so, but there's something about you that's a little too wild to be the steadying influence most schools require.'

She stared back forcefully at that. 'Then why insist on my coming here? I'm not about to turn into someone else overnight.'

'I hope not. What I need here is a companion with sharp-eyed ferocity.'

'I am not ferocious!'

Her outraged denial merely brought a slight smile to his lips and when Alissa glared at him in frustration, his smile broadened. 'Don't be offended, Miss Brent. My whole life is based on my ability to see people for what they are.'

'You didn't do so well with your wife, apparently,' Alissa

pointed out tartly and she was sure that only the entry of Martha with their food stopped him from leaping up and dismissing her on the spot. He was certainly not accustomed to being challenged.

When Martha left the room, he looked at Alissa with narrowed eyes. 'So, you hit back when attacked. I was beginning to worry about your starry-eyed, feminine looks and the fact that you kept shyly out of my way. Now you're back to the person I thought you were, throwing boulders instead of stones. Keep on throwing the boulders, Miss Brent, I can duck.'

Or retaliate, she mused silently, glancing up at him. No, she did not like this man. He was all thought and no heart, except where his children where concerned. He'd probably ruined plenty of firms in his climb to the top and he'd probably been hateful to his wife.

All the same, the story of the attempted abduction was true. She'd been there and seen it with her own eyes.

'I don't know enough,' she suddenly blurted out, staring straight back at him when he looked up. 'It's ridiculous!'

'I told you the story and that's all you need to know.'

'It is *not* all I need to know. It's like being blindfolded. I need to know the enemy if I'm to be properly on guard.'

His eyes narrowed alarmingly. 'I am not about to let you pry into my private life.'

Alissa stared at him in irritation. 'An automaton doesn't have a private life, Mr Tempest. It simply functions. I don't want stories of your wedding and fights with your in-laws. I want photographs, descriptions, and probable lines of attack. For reasons I can't quite fathom, your enemies seem to have become my enemies and I don't intend to be taken by surprise – not even for double the salary!'

The dark brows rose as he regarded her quizzically. 'Did

I actually offer to double your salary? Obviously it's a fault in my "robotic" make-up. When I go in for reprogramming, I'll have to get it fixed.'

Alissa continued to glare at him and he suddenly relaxed, leaning back and looking at her thoughtfully.

'All right. There are photographs somewhere, though I doubt if any are here. I'll search around, however. I felt it necessary to keep a few for the children. One day they may want to see what Cynthia looks like. She's their mother, however inadequate. As to the relatives, I rarely saw them so there are unlikely to be any photographs of them. When Cynthia left she took everything that wasn't nailed down.' He stared at her moodily. 'Being an automaton has its compensations, Miss Brent. As it turned out, James was the one who was hurt, Sally was too young to know.'

'I'm sorry.' Alissa felt the odd compassion surfacing again. 'I can't help hitting back, it's how I'm made. But it seems so unreal. To me, a mother is like my own mother was and like Candy is. There's always the thought at the back of my mind that your wife must want the children back just to be with them.'

'My ex-wife,' he corrected. 'Don't waste your sympathy. Save it for James. If I had the power to have Cynthia shipped to another planet I would do so, her new husband with her.'

It suddenly occurred to Alissa that he was jealous and she resolved to watch her tongue in future. If by any chance he still cared for Cynthia, then that would complicate matters. After all, he must have cared for her once. They had two children. Had their mother willingly left them or had he used his power to cut her from their lives?

She went to bed later still puzzling over the matter. Kieran's handsome face lingered in her mind and beside it, the image of a little boy who was facing his hurt with a silent refusal to soften at all. One day, he too would be like his father but Sally seemed to drift dream-like above it all. She was the lucky one.

Lessons began next day. Alissa had chosen an upstairs room where there would be no noise to disturb them. As she had expected, James was very clever, well in advance of his years. He didn't once ask her advice and everything he did was perfect and correct. Alissa felt very much superfluous and, had it not been for Sally who took up a lot of her time, she would have been left feeling like a fraud.

'I want to go to the beach now.' James slammed his books closed as the morning drew to an end.

Alissa heard the impertinent tone of his voice. She carefully avoided looking up. 'Perhaps when lessons are over. I expect your father will agree to a trip down to the beach if we ask him.'

'You're supposed to be looking after us. You're here so that Dad won't have to bother with us.'

'I'm here to teach you and, obviously, if you're bored, I'll have to make things more difficult. I'm used to much older children and I didn't want to ask too much of you to begin with.'

'A man would have just made his own mind up and taken us to the beach without asking anybody,' James looked up at her with angry eyes, his mouth set stubbornly. 'I wanted a man to come with us and teach me.'

'I like Lissa.' Sally looked upset and Alissa put her arm round the little girl to soothe her. It only served to anger James further.

'Women are useless! I hate women!' He ran out of the room and Sally looked up with round, anxious eyes.

'Will you smack him, Lissa?'

Alissa gave her a quick hug. 'Of course not. I expect something upset him. If you can manage to finish making this duck, I'll go and find him.'

Alissa went quickly out into the upstairs hall but James was not there, neither was he immediately visible in the garden. She had the feeling he had taken his hurt and his temper to his room. When she listened carefully at his closed door, she heard what she had expected to hear – the noise of angry banging about.

She left him to work out his temper. She had something else to do. Somebody had given him this distorted outlook, had taught him that women were useless, and she had a good idea who it was. She went down the stairs with her own temper soaring.

She already knew the location of the room Kieran used as a study and she marched straight there, her anger rising by the minute. Was this how he had explained Cynthia's absence? Women were useless, no good, men were a more preferable species? No wonder James looked at her with resentful eyes.

By the time she reached the study, Alissa was ready for battle and she knocked only very briefly, not even waiting to be invited inside. She was not surprised to find Kieran busy with his moneymaking equipment. He seemed to be surrounded by electronic devices and as she went in, he was just putting the phone down.

Obviously this place was set up permanently so that he could keep his finger on the market wherever he was. The market was not on his mind at the moment, however. He looked quite startled and his expression gave Alissa a feeling of grim satisfaction.

'What's wrong?' He made a move to get up but she was across the room, leaning over his desk to glare before he could quite complete the action.

'Nothing you haven't laid the groundwork for very competently! I suppose James' conviction that women are useless and men are the only ones to be trusted comes from you? I imagine when he says he hates women he's simply aping his father.'

It was a little alarming to see the slow way he stood and to realise that any towering she had been doing was now completely overshadowed by his height and very menacing presence. It was also rather frightening to see the surprise change, not to his normal indifferent expression but to red-hot anger.

'You think I set out to teach James what I've learned the hard way? You imagine I plan to ruin his outlook on life by making snide comments about the members of your sex? I deliberately keep women on my staff to soften his life, not to use as an example of what to avoid.' He came round the desk to stand close and blaze at her more effectively. 'Anything that James thinks about women he decided all by himself. A very important woman in his life deserted him but she did a lot more before then. Going away was the only kind thing she ever did for my son!'

'He stormed out of the room for no reason at all,' Alissa began, somewhat chastened by both his words and his anger.

'Then storm after him and get the situation under control. If you can't get the better of one small boy then you're not much of a teacher and neither are you much of a woman.'

'I can get the better of anyone,' Alissa flared. 'Circumstances are not normal here though. I don't know what rules to follow when you haven't laid down any rules.'

'Make your own decisions and make up your own rules,' he growled, turning away as the telephone rang.

'Fine! Then we'll go to the beach immediately after lunch.

That was what this little contretemps was about. At least it was his excuse to show his dislike of the female of the species.'

'You're going to give in every time he throws a tantrum?' His hand was on the phone but he let it continue to ring as he gave her a disgusted look.

'I won't have to give in. I'll have him eating out of my hand before long. I can come at this sneakily.'

Alissa spun round to go but he gave a sudden low laugh and when she turned angrily, she was not pleased to see real amusement on his face.

'I can't imagine you coming at anything sneakily, Miss Brent. You're more likely to rush in wielding a weapon, even if it's only your sharp tongue.' He reached towards the phone again, dismissing her. 'It's safe on the beach. Just warn me if you plan to go further afield.'

Alissa marched back to the door but she knew he was still watching her, probably with a superior look on his face. He was still letting the phone ring. She looked round with narrow-eyed annoyance.

'Better answer the phone,' she suggested, gleefully insubordinate. 'You might lose a million while you're wasting your time with me.'

'They'll ring again. I'm too important to be ignored.'

His arrogance infuriated her even more and she was not one bit ashamed that she had misjudged him as far as James was concerned.

'I don't like you, Mr Tempest!'

'I remember,' he assured her in a soft, silky voice. 'Nevertheless, you're working for me and, as I seem to be paying you double rates, I suggest you get on with it. Save your violence for dinner when I have more time to deal with you.'

The last word as usual – neatly said – and she knew quite

well that she skirted on the edge of violence every time she spoke to him. The unexpected bursts of passion were a quirk of her nature.

She left without looking back and was disgusted to realise that the phone was still ringing patiently. Some poor secretary somewhere would be sitting with her heart pounding anxiously in case she missed him and got herself dismissed for incompetence.

Pretending a total disregard for anything Kieran might think, Alissa immediately took the children to the beach with a packed lunch. Martha was happy to accommodate her wishes and as she left the house with the children in tow, Alissa was still fuming silently. She was not used to working under these sorts of circumstances. School was a tranquil place and her stay in France had been a delightful experience even though it had been without any sort of adventure.

During the course of this morning, she had found herself wishing more than once she had taken up Candy's offer and moved in with them for a period of smothering. She was not even free to think her own thoughts in this place because, in some mysterious way, Kieran Tempest seemed to be constantly at the front of her mind. Coming here had not been one of her better ideas.

The children ran ahead. James was subdued and, in spite of her annoyance, Alissa felt pity for him. However clever, he was still just a little boy and his hurt was almost tangible. If anyone was going to feel the sharp edge of her tongue it was definitely going to be Kieran Tempest and not this child who had already suffered enough.

'Hold up,' she called, as the children seemed to be intent on going for miles. 'Let's settle here to eat and then you can show me all your secret places on the beach. I feel quite lost.'

They both stopped to watch her as she came towards them.

With a wrap-around cotton dress over her bikini she felt relatively secure from any unwanted prying eyes and she ignored the way James stared at her with an unreadable, dark expression.

'You're tall for a girl,' he suddenly pointed out as she put down the lunch basket and prepared to settle by them.

'True,' she agreed, sitting on the sand and diving into the secrets of the packed lunch. 'I've stopped growing now though. I won't get any taller.'

'Is that why he chose you, because you're tall?' James had the intent look of his father about him. 'I know you're here to guard us. I expect you're with the police.'

'Good try, but wrong,' Alissa assured him, unable to stop the grin that came to her face. 'I'm a teacher. I don't think tall had anything to do with your father choosing me.'

'It's because you're beautiful,' Sally ventured loyally and Alissa's grin widened.

'Thank you, but that's not why he chose me either. He chose me because I'm fierce,' she confided, addressing her last remarks to James. 'I have a wild temper. Your father thinks that's good, under the circumstances.'

'The nanny screamed,' James said with a slightly scornful curl to his lips.

'Hmm,' Alissa mused, handing out food to each of them. 'I would be more inclined to shout and fight. I don't like to lose a battle.'

'I don't expect there'll be a battle. This is a secret place,' James looked round at the beach and the distant volcano. 'Nobody knows about Antarra.'

'I know about Antarra,' Sally piped up indignantly and James gave her a pitying look.

'Of course you do, silly. You're one of us. Nobody knows about this place but us. Uncle Carl doesn't know, so he's going to be wasting his time looking for us at home. If anyone gets close to the house, we'll know about it.'

Alissa ate in silence. Still a little stunned at this odd conversation. James had talked neatly around the point without actually saying anything outright. She knew she was being summed up very quietly. He was weighing her useful-ness against her nuisance value. It was alarming to be scrutinised so professionally by an eight-year-old child. He would be exactly like his father if she didn't do something about it.

'I thought volcanic islands had dark sand,' Alissa said as they finished lunch and sat for a moment looking out to sea.

'It's dark at the other side of the island,' James answered. 'It's almost black in places, not nearly as nice as it is here. Dad says it's because all the past eruptions have been at the other side. If it ever comes this way, we'll not have nice clean sand afterwards.'

The idea was not at all pleasing and Alissa gave a quick glance at Sally who was digging away quietly and not really taking any of this in.

'Your father says the volcano is dormant.'

'Dormant but not dead,' James corrected, still gazing out to sea. 'Dormant means sleeping, I think.'

'It does. Let's hope it's always comfortably asleep. The thought of it waking up is not to my liking at all.'

'I thought you liked to fight battles?' He pounced on her slip in an uncannily adult way.

'I don't *like* to fight battles but if there is a battle, I'll not run away. However,' she added, 'I don't like the idea of chal-lenging an erupting volcano to a fight. So let's hope it goes on sleeping.'

James suddenly gave her an unexpectedly amused smile and she knew his mind was working. He was utterly composed and she felt uncomfortably aware that a lot was going on in that clever little head which she didn't know about.

One good thing had come of this expedition though. He was talking to her. It was a cautious, tentative beginning and some of his words were because he was setting traps to catch her out but, nonetheless, he was talking.

Kieran had watched the start of the expedition to the beach. He stared through the open window at the sight of his children and this beautiful, lithe, irritating woman who swung along with a picnic basket on her arm while Sally skipped beside her like a contented puppy. Contentment was not something his children were used to. It was not something he could offer, in spite of his love for them.

James walked in silence, his very stance indicative of his stiffly guarded attitude. Alissa Brent wouldn't manage to get around James and Kieran wondered whether any woman could win him over. A soft and gentle female would find herself despised. James would fight any woman who ordered him about. What attitude would this new addition to his life take?

Kieran frowned as he watched her graceful walk, vastly irritated to find his eyes lingering on her slender figure. He was remembering her words, as clean and sharp as a knife, 'I don't like you, Mr Tempest.'

That had stung. And it had been surprisingly hurtful. Plenty of people didn't like him but Alissa Brent was too close for comfort. Still, he hadn't engaged her services for her charm. She was here as an extra pair of eyes. In all probability a policewoman would have been better, but he needed a teacher for the children and he had no doubt that Alissa Brent was a very good teacher.

In any case, there was nothing he could do about it now. They were here until he tracked down Carl and traced him back to Cynthia. Everything was now in motion. A few more days and he would know. Every spare man he had was on the job, as well as a few he could not really spare. Meanwhile he was stuck with Alissa Brent and so was James, like it or not.

He turned away from the window, frowning when he realised just how much she had got under his skin. He had a sudden wish that she'd been ugly and dowdy, not someone with those long silky legs and that slender figure. He would have to ignore her but she was about as easy to ignore as the volcano. And just as dangerous too.

It was only as they were coming back to the house that Alissa realised that they had been under observation all the time. The gardener had clearly moved with his work to make it possible to keep them visible. Alissa's first reaction of annoyance faded as she acknowledged that they had come here for safety and that Kieran would have to take whatever measures he saw fit to assure himself that they were indeed safe.

The children seemed to have noticed nothing unusual and in many ways it had been a very successful trip. James said little but his face was not quite so tight and, from time to time, he regarded her with interested eyes instead of the downright hostility he had shown from the first.

At bedtime she kissed Sally goodnight but when she moved to offer James the same comfort, his dark eyes warned her that this would go down very badly. Alissa grinned at him and ruffled his hair. She was prepared to bide her time and, as she turned at the door, she observed that James had a smile on his face, even though his eyes were determinedly shut.

As she got ready for dinner, Alissa realised she'd been

touched by the sun more than usual. There was a flush to her face that enhanced the colour of her eyes and gave her skin a healthy glow. A few more days on the beach and she would look as if she had been on a very expensive holiday.

It would have seemed quite like a holiday, in fact, had it not been a run for cover. As things were, this was merely a hiding place until Kieran had sorted out his problems. When that would be she had no idea. She didn't know either what action he was taking in his silent way but she imagined he was not merely staying here and keeping his head down. That was not within his character.

By now, Alissa wasn't sure what his character was. One thing she did know, he was not the mechanical figure she had formerly thought. Sometimes there was a look on his face that was almost sadness. That always touched her and made her sorry for her hasty remarks.

Sometimes he laughed unexpectedly as if he found her amusing. He didn't look harsh then and she always found herself thinking that she had misjudged him. Then he would say something that infuriated her. This drove her instantly into her rock-throwing mode.

It boiled down to this. She didn't understand him.

chapter five

At dinnertime, Alissa decided to try enthusiasm mixed with a slight touch of friendliness. It was better than spending the day dreading the evening to come, when the children were in bed. As far as she could see, she had two choices. She could eat and scuttle off quickly to her own room or she could talk to her employer.

She had no intention of trying to charm him into being slightly more human. She was well aware that this was impossible but for the sake of her own comfort, it would perhaps be better to bend a little and not continue with her aggressive and defiant stance.

Her soft, blue dress was extremely feminine and, to her mind, almost verging on the boring. Normally she would have teamed this dress with high heels, a smart summer jacket and huge earrings. Tonight she wore dainty sandals and no earrings at all.

She sighed as she observed herself through the mirror. Exceedingly demure, not like her at all. She would have to alter her tone of voice to match and act accordingly. Maybe it would be worth it. She had some misgivings about that but it was worth a try.

Kieran noticed her more feminine attire and her altered attitude the moment she walked into the room. He regarded her with sardonic suspicion and Alissa knew at once that she'd made a big mistake. There was no getting round this man and she had been foolish to think otherwise. He looked at the world with his silver grey eyes and that brain clicked smoothly into action.

Still, she'd planned it, dressed for the part, and she was not about to abandon the idea without trying. He ate in silence and ignored her.

'We had a very nice time on the beach today,' she ventured brightly when his silence began to get on her nerves.

'Good.'

'James talked to me,' she persisted, refusing to allow her annoyance to surface.

'I didn't expect he would continue to be offensive. His attitude is rather stiff for an eight-year-old boy but, normally, he is scrupulously polite.'

'I didn't for one moment mean to suggest that he was offensive in any way,' Alissa said, biting back her normal sharp rejoinder. 'I'm merely pointing out that things are progressing in as much as he is now speaking to me, more or less normally.'

'I imagined things would progress, Miss Brent. Your qualifications are impeccable. A good teacher will always get around her charges. That's why I chose the best.'

'I imagined you chose me for my fierce qualities,' Alissa reminded him, even more irritated by his manner and his rather patronising attitude. He had never looked up from his meal either and that seemed to be indicative of his cold, dismissive disposition.

He looked up then, allowing his gaze to run over her like someone contemplating a new piece of furniture.

'Perhaps I made a mistake. You look anything but fierce tonight. You look decidedly feminine.'

'That may be something to do with the fact that I'm female,' Alissa snapped, unable to keep up her conciliatory attitude.

'You seem to be subtly emphasising that, Miss Brent. No jewellery, a soft little dress, demure hairstyle.' He gave what she took to be a nasty smile. 'Did you intend to circumnavigate my hostility by any chance?'

'Not even with a battleship! I'm attempting to be civilised. Where you're concerned it doesn't come easy to me. But I'll not try it again. Goodnight, Mr Tempest!'

Alissa stood and walked out of the room, leaving the rest of her meal. It was either eat it and choke or toss it over his arrogant head. He did well to mention the word 'offensive'. She had never met anyone so completely offensive in her whole life! As far as she could see, he didn't have one single redeeming feature. He could be as handsome as the devil but he was utterly abominable.

She stormed into her room and kicked off her sandals. She had to curb the wish to throw them at the wall. All she felt now, besides furious, was stupid. She had tried friendliness but it had been looked upon as weakness or, even worse, some sort of trick. He must live a very miserable life if he viewed all approaches of a friendly nature as trickery.

She grimaced with annoyance. Of course he didn't have a miserable life. He was as rich as Croesus, with everyone bending over backwards to pander to his every whim.

Alissa walked out on to the balcony of her room and stood looking into the night. It was velvet dark, balmy and tropical. The sea was a glittering carpet of movement against the shore, the silver-edged waves caught in the faint light of the moon. It was beautiful here and peaceful. At least, it would have been peaceful if she didn't have a cleverly made android to deal with.

A red glow lit the sky to her left and a faint wisp of smoke rose into the night air. The volcano was stirring in its sleep and she didn't know enough about volcanoes to understand whether she should be afraid or merely interested. She didn't know whether the fire meant anything or not.

She consoled herself with the thought that there were villages on the slopes of the volcano and there was no sign that anyone else was uneasy. This probably happened all the time. If she had known there was a volcano, she would have looked up some information about volcanic habits. But she had not even had the sense to insist on knowing where Antarra was before she came here.

Looking back she realised she had been particularly stupid. She had done something she would not have recommended to anyone else. She had let her heart rule her head and this was where it had got her.

The fire came again, a throbbing red glow with the aftermath of white smoke lingering on the darkened sky and Alissa felt a real burst of anxiety. From her first sight of it, the volcano had made her uneasy. Whatever she was doing, it seemed to be at the back of her mind like some premonition and she was incapable of looking on it as part of the landscape.

A knock on her door made Alissa feel guilty. She sincerely hoped it was not Martha Gregson coming to ask if she was ill because of the rejected food on her plate.

'Come in,' she called warily, quickly trying to find an excuse for her precipitous departure from the dining room.

It was Kieran and he took her at her word, coming straight into the room and letting the door swing shut behind him.

'If you wished to speak to me, I would have been quite willing to come to your study,' Alissa told him in a tight voice as she drew herself up like a guard on duty. She wished she still had her shoes on. 'Any reprimand would have carried more weight in formal surroundings.'

'If you prefer, we could go down to my study and you can reprimand me there. I was hoping you'd finished being annoyed with me though. I came to apologise for my remarks.'

'Your offensive remarks,' Alissa corrected, eyeing him severely.

'My offensive remarks,' he conceded. 'I can only offer as an excuse that I'm extremely suspicious of women.'

'Then why didn't you get a man instead of me?'

'Sally needs a woman, a woman who will love her and bring some warmth into her life. James needs that too but he's not ready to admit it yet.'

Once again, Alissa felt the treacherous softening of her heart towards this man. Who brought warmth into his life? Who brought love? Did he turn with a suspicious reaction on anyone who was even slightly pleasant?

'I'm sorry, Miss Brent. I don't really intend to make your life uncomfortable here.'

'You don't make it uncomfortable,' Alissa assured him. 'You just annoy me. Tonight I really tried to be normal with you but I came to the conclusion that you don't recognise normality at all. I suppose it's all the business dealings you have.'

'And my past? You can say it, Miss Brent. I won't snap your head off.'

'If you do, I'll only snap back as you know very well,' Alissa reminded him. She turned to look out of the window again and gave a sigh. 'It's not working out too well, is it? You didn't take into account when you decided you wanted someone fierce that I would also fight back with you. You made a mistake and, if you want to admit it, I'm quite prepared to go back home and forget the whole thing.'

'You can't. You now know where we are.'

'There you go again,' Alissa snapped as she spun round to face him. 'Do you imagine I would try to find your brother-in-law and guide him here? What sort of life do you live when you don't trust anyone?'

'A safe life.'

'A miserable life.'

He stood looking at her in silence. Then he asked, 'Do you want to go?'

She turned away again, giving another deep sigh of resignation. 'If I had my head screwed on tightly I would say "yes" very speedily. As it is, the answer is no. I don't want to go. I want to help the children. I imagine they've had quite enough desertion in their lives. I won't add to that. I'm not running out.'

'Thank you. You're quite remarkable.'

'I'm quite foolish I expect,' Alissa murmured. The volcano flared again. There was no sound, just a little flash of fire and she stood watching it intently. 'That bothers me a bit,' she confessed.

'El Bueno? It's perfectly safe.' He came to stand beside her and looked across at the dark shape against the sky. 'It lets off steam from time to time.'

'Is that its name, El Bueno?'

'They call it that in the village. I don't know if it has any other name but El Bueno means…'

'The good one,' Alissa finished for him. 'Why that name?'

'Volcanic soil is very fertile. Good crops grow on the slopes and nobody can remember the last explosion. It was many centuries ago, so they tend to regard the volcano with pleasure and not with fear.'

'How do they know it's not going to suddenly become the bad one?'

'They rely on the experts.' Kieran looked down at her. 'We have an expert out here at the moment. George Gregson was telling me this morning that there's a man in the village who flew in a few days before us.'

'Can you be sure he's what he says he is?' Alissa turned quickly to look at him. 'How do we know he's not with the enemy?'

'Because he's been here before,' Kieran said, impressed by her instant suspicion.

'Hmm.' Alissa turned away. 'I'm getting to be almost as bad as you.'

'Another person with apparently no feelings? I doubt it. You're as full of fire as the volcano. Heat like that would be damaging if you were a mechanical automaton. However, if you're really concerned about the volcano, I can get this expert to call and tell you about it.'

Alissa turned on him with real enthusiasm. 'Would you? It would be wonderful for the children to learn about it from someone who really knows.'

'Bring the expert into school you mean? My suggestion was not to educate the children. It was intended to set your mind at rest.'

'Well, there's nothing wrong with killing two birds with one stone is there? There's no reason for the children to know I'm anxious and they can learn at the same time.'

'I'll fix it up,' he promised, turning to leave. 'It's a little late to hide things from James though. When I saw him tonight, he asked me to tell you that there's nothing to worry about as far as the volcano is concerned. He said you seemed to be scared of it.'

'I suppose he thinks that's typical of a woman, another black mark against me.'

'As a matter of fact,' Kieran said, turning back to look at her. 'James was a little concerned. He seemed to think you might decide to leave. Apparently you told him you were not fierce enough to fight a volcano head-on. I rather imagine he was handing that particular task over to me. I fight the mountain and you tackle everyone else.'

'You mean he doesn't want me to leave?'

'I rather think not. At any rate, he feels the need to protect you. I suspect you bring out the male in him. He pointed out that you were quite tall for a girl.'

'I know,' Alissa admitted with a rueful smile. 'He thought I was a policewoman.'

Kieran actually laughed, a quite normal laugh. 'You didn't consider letting him go on thinking that?'

'I did not. The truth is sacred to a child and little lies lead to big lies. If I'd allowed him to think that, he would have felt betrayed and foolish when he found out the truth. Children feel embarrassed quite easily. Anyway,' she added, 'I don't tell lies. It complicates life and makes you feel like a criminal.'

'You're astonishing,' Kieran murmured, glancing down at her. 'Most women lie.'

'They don't. You can have no grounds for saying that. It's prejudice and James can do without prejudice. How many women have you known who lied?'

'My wife.'

'She lied to you?' Alissa felt again the softening inside her, the pity.

'All the time. But don't start feeling sorry for me, Miss Brent. Believe me, she paid for it.'

Kieran said goodnight again, closing the door as he left and Alissa turned back to gaze at the volcano, the mountain with fire in its hair. What an empty life he led, even with all his intelligence and his wealth. She wondered how much Cynthia had paid and in what manner. Cynthia had lost her children, for one thing, and had lost this way of life. Alissa suddenly wanted to know a lot more about Kieran's ex-wife. She wondered how much Martha Gregson knew and if she would talk.

A couple of days later, Alissa got the chance to speak privately to Martha. Instead of confronting her outright, she decided to try a more tactful approach and refused to acknowledge that it was also a trifle sneaky. She spent the next two days cultivating Martha's company, chatting to her on every conceivable pretext. She was learning to be diplomatic in this household and she satisfied her conscience by telling herself that she really needed to know about the children's mother.

'Yes, I knew her,' Martha admitted, with slightly tightened lips. 'She's a very glamorous woman with about enough moral standards to put in a small paper bag.'

'Did she ever come here?'

'No. Never. Mr Tempest bought this place after the divorce. There's always somebody trying to pry into his life, trying to see how he makes all that money.' She gave a snort of annoyance. 'He makes it by being clever but there's always some people who try to do things by sneaking up on others. Anyway, Mr Tempest needed a hiding-place, a place where he didn't have to watch his back, so he bought this house. Of course we go into the village but, mainly, everything we want comes here by boat.'

'Does Mr Tempest ever go into the village?' Alissa decided it was not wise to persist about Cynthia.

'I haven't noticed him going there but I expect he does occasionally.'

'So he's all alone? What a pity.'

'Well, there's Mrs Fox,' Martha Gregson said thoughtfully. 'George and I often wonder about that. He must be keen on her because she comes to the house and not many people call here. She's got a house on the other side of the island.'

Alissa made herself a cup of coffee and went to start afternoon lessons. Nothing much had been learned after all, except the bit about Mrs Fox. One thing had become clear though. She was wasting her sympathies on a Kieran who, in all probability, was not lonely at all, not if he had Mrs Fox.

'You live and you learn,' Alissa muttered to herself. She was vaguely irritated and almost wished she hadn't tried to get information from Martha.

How trustworthy was Mrs Fox, especially with a name like that? And why hadn't she offered to look out for the children? Surely she could have coped for just a short while? Was he keeping company with a married lady or was she divorced like him? She may be a widow, of course. It was none of Alissa's business. She wouldn't meet the woman anyway so there was little use in pondering about it.

Carl Henderson sat back and looked round the club. With its leather chairs, mahogany tables and subdued lighting it was a comfortable, civilised place to be in. He felt at home here. He could get used to this sort of thing. He doubted if he would be offered lunch but it was easy enough to daydream about it – white cloths, excellent silver and glass, the pheasant, the wine. The dreams were wide except that they did invariably end with his favourite daydream, stepping out of the club, well-fed and satisfied, to return to his high-rise office in the city.

It would have been possible if Cynthia hadn't cheated on Tempest. And what a little worm to cheat with! Emile, whose second name he couldn't pronounce, a supposed count from some obscure central European country. Pigs might fly! Emile looked as if he might have more likely escaped from some central European jail.

Carl Henderson had never liked Tempest. In fact, a shiver of apprehension assailed him every time he thought about the man, but Cynthia's present husband was a slimy little toad of some sort, all teeth and shiny black hair that was too long. If his sister had stayed with Tempest, this club might have been a possibility. Something in the City might have been a possibility too.

Not that Carl knew anything about money matters other than that money was a good, sound commodity, especially for spending. Still, Tempest might have relented and offered some sort of position in his vast moneyed empire. Cynthia had put paid to all that though. There were other ways, however, and this was one of them.

Having been shown to his seat by a portly butler of some sort, he waited for the man who might just lead him to the start of his fortunes. Henderson closed his eyes for a moment to let the quiet affluence of this expensive club for businessmen flow over him.

'Henderson.' The voice roused him from his dreams of wealth and Carl Henderson sat up straight, instantly irritated by the patronising tone of the man who now sat facing him. Here was another wealthy man Carl didn't like. Not as wealthy as the man *had* been – courtesy of Tempest. That's what this was all about. Cynthia's ex-husband had all but put Bloomdale out of business.

Looking at him now, Henderson wondered if Cyril Bloomdale had been pushed over the edge by it all. He didn't exactly look as if he was in full possession of his faculties. Carl Henderson knew all about him – inherited wealth, much of it lost in idiotic schemes and even more idiotic gambling on the Stock Exchange. Questionable practices, like one of those dark and ugly fish that stay deep down and pursue their dirty ways.

Kieran Tempest had swooped in like a hungry, white shark and almost wiped him out. It had been rumoured that it was an old score being settled.

Carl wondered if Tempest considered the matter closed. After all, Tempest hadn't wiped Bloomdale out completely. He decided that *he* would have wiped Bloomdale out altogether if he had been the white shark. What did they call that terrifying creature, the ultimate fighting machine? It just about described Tempest.

'So, what have you discovered?' Bloomdale asked in his million-pound voice.

'They're on an island. It's called Antarra. A few miles off the Mexican coast, very few Europeans, mostly just the islanders, a mixture of Spanish descent, farmers.'

'Farmers. Hmm. No problem there.' Bloomdale fixed him with rather alarming eyes, weird, pale blue, behind thick spectacles. They looked like two glass eyes because of their utter lack of expression. It was an uncomfortable experience to face the man, heavy body, fat white hands and two glassy eyes that looked right through you. Yes, Henderson decided. Bloomdale was mad. Not that it mattered, money was money and invariably he needed it. Besides, he didn't like Tempest.

'Having allowed yourself to be outwitted by a small boy and a screaming nanny who is little more than a girl, you have now located the quarry. We must hope for more efficiency this time.'

Carl Henderson squirmed in his seat, harsh words bitten back. He wanted to swear at this fat, overfed gargoyle that looked as if he'd escaped from a nearby mental institution. Instead he sat in silence. Money, after all, was money.

'I shall not invite you to stay for lunch,' Bloomdale was saying. 'Being seen with you is not wise at all but at least there's safety in this club. I would not feel safe meeting you on your own territory. Now that you have located them, the plan can be set in motion again. See to it. The financing of this affair is no problem. Funds are already in place as we speak. Good morning, Mr Henderson.'

He stood and walked out of the room, leaving Henderson to find his own way. When this was over, there were ways of dealing with that type. He had a few acquaintances who could pick Bloomdale off with ease.

But first things first. There was the boy and Tempest. It was almost laughable the way he had been able to charm the information he needed out of Mrs Dobson at the agency. Following Tempest that day had been no problem and she had been so sympathetic when Carl had moaned about his regret at not getting Miss Brent for his own children.

Yes, he had played the part of exhausted businessman very well. Even so, he no longer felt at home in this exclusive club. That was Bloomdale's fault. He could afford to wait though. Insults would be repaid in full. But first, Tempest.

The next day, Kieran called Alissa to his study to tell her he had set up a meeting with the volcano expert.

'I invited him to dinner tonight. If you use your powers of persuasion you might get him to fly you over the volcano. You can get a good look then.'

'Right over the centre of it?' Alissa looked quite aghast. 'I wouldn't dare. Suppose we came down and...'

Kieran was laughing, to her surprise and chagrin. 'I thought you were daring?'

'I'm not foolhardy. I'm prepared to meet trouble if it comes, but I'm not prepared to go out and find it wilfully. Nobody in their right mind would challenge a volcano.'

'Let's wait and see what he says,' Kieran advised and she thought she detected a slightly soothing note in his voice, which was all right providing it wasn't patronising.

'Well, there's no danger in talking to him, he's only a man.'

'Very true. No problem at all.' Kieran was looking at her with amusement and Alissa gave him a scathing glance as she marched off.

When Alissa went down to dinner that night, the man was having a drink with Kieran. At first glance he appeared to be quite stockily built although he was much taller than Alissa. She realised it was because he was standing beside Kieran and there was such a contrast between the two men.

The newcomer was deeply tanned and looked as if he spent a great deal of time out of doors. His bright blue eyes looked sharp and interested, again the sort of eyes a man would have if he spent most of his time in the open air.

'Andrew Dodds,' Kieran introduced them as Alissa stopped and looked slightly anxious. She had forgotten they were having a visitor and Kieran noted the fact with a sardonic twist to his mouth. 'This is our volcano expert, Miss Brent. He's quite prepared to be questioned at some length.'

'I hear you're a little uneasy about El Bueno, Miss Brent,' Andrew Dodds said, grinning at her. 'I'll see if I can set your mind at rest.'

'I was hoping you would tell the children about it but unfortunately they're in bed now. Is there any chance of you coming again during the daytime do you think?' Alissa gave him a bright smile in the rather forlorn hope that it would annoy Kieran, who was looking particularly smug. She was very much aware of his important presence.

'Sure. Name the day. I could go on talking about volcanoes forever,' Andrew Dodds told her cheerfully.

'What about tomorrow? You can tell me all the really worrying things tonight and tell the children the exciting bits tomorrow.'

'There's nothing to worry about,' Kieran interrupted, his piercing eyes subduing Alissa.

'Not at the moment,' Andrew agreed. 'We monitor things fairly well. Of course, from time to time the unexpected event occurs.'

Alissa questioned him anxiously as they went in to dinner. 'What unexpected event?'

'Almost anything. That's what makes volcanoes so fascinating.' He was sitting next to Alissa and he turned enthusiastically to look at her. 'Don't forget the power we're talking about here, the pressure. There's constant movement in the earth. The comfortable thought that we're on a nice hard ball spinning in space is totally erroneous. The magma, molten rock, moves inside, deep down. There are earthquakes down there, the seismometers pick them up five miles beneath the earth's surface. Earthquakes like these are important and possibly the least threatening. There are about fifty volcanic eruptions a year worldwide.'

Alissa glanced at Kieran and he didn't look particularly pleased.

'You actually like doing this for a living?'

'Wouldn't do anything else. Can't think about much else either.'

'I wouldn't be able to sleep,' Alissa muttered, getting on with her meal. 'What do you call yourself?'

'Andy,' he said promptly.

Alissa suppressed a wild giggle. 'I mean your title.'

'Oh, I'm a Vulcanologist.' There was a certain amount of pride in his voice.

Alissa looked up at him with the necessary amount of awe. 'Really? It sounds almost alien.'

'I suppose I am alien,' he agreed with a boyish shrug. 'I'm usually flying over volcanoes making aerial surveys or climbing up them.'

Alissa glanced up at him. 'Suppose they suddenly just go

off with a bang?'

'Catastrophic eruptions without warning are, fortunately, very rare, although the Columbo volcano erupted just one day after the scientists said there was no danger. Hot mudflows killed twenty-two thousand people.'

Alissa was beginning to think she didn't really want to know anything else and Kieran looked like a savage who was trying to remember his manners and finding it difficult.

'Volcanoes that erupt infrequently tend to erupt violently,' Andrew continued with a look of great pleasure. 'Of course,' he added, 'the pyroclastic flow is as dangerous as the mud slides, more so even.'

'The what?' Her dazed voice matched her feelings. Hadn't this man come to allay her fears rather than stir them up?

'Pyroclastic flow. That's dense avalanches of rock, ash and gas. It moves at about a hundred miles an hour and burns everything in its path.'

'Pompeii,' Alissa decided glumly, wishing she hadn't asked.

'Exactly!'

'Perhaps we should change the subject,' Kieran insisted in a quiet but authoritative voice after a keen glance at Alissa's face. 'I don't think this is setting Miss Brent's mind at rest.'

'Sorry. Am I frightening you?' Andrew Dodds looked astonished. 'There's really nothing to worry about with old Bueno. If you like, I'll fly you over it and let you get a close look.'

'Er…I rarely get any time off,' Alissa said quickly. 'The children you know. Mr Tempest is very busy and I'm here to teach them and take care of them. I can't just go flying off like that.'

'You can have time off whenever you like,' Kieran assured her with a very amused look that showed a desire to taunt.

'Don't forget though that you're often air sick,' he added, softening when she looked at him in horror.

'Yes, that's true,' Alissa lied quickly. 'I can be quite a nuisance.'

'She can indeed,' Kieran agreed solemnly, his lips twisting in a wry smile when she shot him a look of deep annoyance.

'So when shall I come to talk to the children,' Andrew Dodds asked later as he was leaving.

'I'll work out a schedule,' Alissa promised. 'They're both very small and having listened to you, I doubt if you could get down to their level. We had no idea that you had such serious expertise, did we?' She appealed to Kieran. The children would be scared out of their wits. She was!

'Yes, that's true,' Kieran agreed firmly. 'Alissa will have to get around to working them up to it with pictures and things.'

'Er…fire birds and tales like that,' Alissa improvised wildly, greatly regretting her eager acceptance of Kieran's decision to have an expert to dinner.

Andrew looked a little startled at the suggestion of fire birds. He was totally involved with volcanoes at a high level and the idea of reducing their status to legends and stories refused to seep into his head.

'Well, let me know,' he said as he left.

'We will,' Kieran assured him with what Alissa took to be a rather grim smile.

She retreated to the drawing room and he followed her in, after assuring Martha that she could clear up and go.

'Not one of my better ideas,' he muttered as he walked forward and poured himself a drink. Without asking, he poured Alissa a small brandy and handed it to her. She took it almost without thought and sipped it with an anxiety that was utterly foreign to her.

'He knew his subject,' she murmured, casting a deeply suspicious glance at the window and seeing the pulsing red glow where El Bueno stood darkly against the night sky.

'He was supposed to set your mind at rest, not scare you senseless. He certainly can't come to tell the children anything.'

'Agreed,' Alissa said. 'Anyway, he's too involved with his own subject. He wouldn't manage to get anything through to them that they could understand.'

'He's suffering from expertosis,' Kieran growled, looking up at her quickly when she giggled and then clamped her lips shut rapidly.

'He's not made you hysterical, has he?' Kieran enquired with an anxious glance at her amused face.

'Not yet. Maybe next time.'

'There won't be a next time. There shouldn't have been a first time. I'm sorry, Alissa. I shouldn't have let you in for that.'

For the second time this evening, he used her name. She imagined it was meant to soothe her. Instead she had this urgent desire to stare morbidly at the volcano. It was taking all her willpower to keep her eyes from it and her head turned towards Kieran.

He switched off the lights, leaving two lamps on and then he turned toward her and nodded at the window. 'Come on. Take a good look and then try to put it out of your mind.'

'I can tell you now that it's just not possible,' she said, walking with him to stand and look at the velvet black of the night sky and the frequent flaring of the volcano. 'I wish we'd decided to hide in Scotland or somewhere. Why don't you own an island there? You'd make a good laird and you could have had all your men lining the coast with claymores in case of invasion by the enemy.'

'A nice thought,' he said with a quiet laugh. 'We had to leave fast though and I just didn't have time to buy a Scottish island and get rid of all the inhabitants. I'll be more prepared in future.'

'Do you think they'll try again?' Alissa looked up at him in the soft light.

'Perhaps.' He glanced down at her and his eyes lingered on her beautiful face. 'Want to desert the ship?'

'No. I just want to escape the volcano,' Alissa assured him with another anxious glance at El Bueno. 'I worked out while he was talking that I can't run at a hundred miles an hour with James under one arm and Sally under the other. I'd much rather take on your relatives single-handed.'

'The only relatives I have are in this house,' Kieran stated with an abrupt return to his chilly attitude. 'Goodnight, Miss Brent,' he finished as he turned to the door. 'I'll leave you with your nightmares.'

'Damned unfeeling android!' Alissa muttered angrily to herself as the door closed behind him. 'And don't think you scare me, Kieran Tempest. Unfriendly men do not worry me. I'm concentrating all my attention on the possibility of fire.'

She returned to her uneasy contemplation of El Bueno and then decided that bed was the best place. She could close her eyes there and, with a bit of luck, she could sleep the worry away.

She climbed the stairs to her room with her shoes in her hand and a grumpy attitude in her mind. Tonight, Kieran had almost been human. Not quite though. He had rescued her from the expert, been prepared to try and set her mind at rest about the volcano but then, of course, he had to spoil it all by reverting to type.

Just one word, just one, and he was back to his frozen attitude. All she had mentioned was relatives, a very innocuous remark. But he had instantly crackled like an iceman and then he had swept out with his final nasty remark.

He was abominable. She didn't like him. She certainly didn't like him any more now than when she'd first set eyes on him. He was a cold, handsome and supremely arrogant man, who took a delight in moving people like chess pieces in his mechanical brain. What was there to like?

He was just crossing the upstairs hall at that moment and his eyes swept over her as they usually did. His attention deepened when he saw her bare feet and her shoes swinging from her hand.

'Sore feet?' he enquired. 'Or are you getting ready for a sprint?'

Alissa tightened her lips and blew hot air through her nose like a bull. It was either that or rush at him head down and bowl him over. With great self-restraint, she said nothing and marched along to her room with aloof dignity. When she cast a scathing glance at him, he was grinning all over his superior face.

Only the thought of the sleeping children prevented Alissa from slamming her door and giving it a hard kick as she did so.

chapter six

Around the back of the house there was a beautiful swimming pool. It was sculptured to a shape that blended with the sweep of the garden. The pale blue tiles made the clear water seem shimmering blue also but Alissa had no urge to rest and languish by the water, even though flowering bushes grew close by and pretty scarlet blooms hung low over the pool in seductive places.

She was an expert swimmer and had been since childhood. Her mother still kept all the medals and cups she had won as a teenager. They were still displayed proudly on a special shelf her father had made. A pool meant swimming, diving and enjoyment of an athletic nature to her, not a place to display bronzed limbs and tiny bikinis.

Having discovered this pool of her dreams, Alissa swam every day with the children. James was a very competent swimmer and she was teaching Sally to swim, whilst keeping an eye on him and urging him to greater expertise.

'I'm tired now,' Sally complained one afternoon after a hard lesson. Alissa lifted her out and dried her off, giving her hair a good rub with a towel until the glowing curls stood out around her face like the petals of a flower.

'Promise to sit here and not move for a few minutes,' Alissa said. 'I want to swim by myself for a while.'

'All right. I promise.' Sally smiled up in the usual sweet way and Alissa beamed at her. She was getting very fond of the children and if James could just be a little more open with her then she would really enjoy being here – except for Kieran and the volcano!

She walked to the deep end of the pool and dived in cleanly. It was something she did very well and when she surfaced, James was out of the water and watching her with deep interest.

'Can you show me how to do that?'

He asked this with the sort of careful probing in his voice that came from a child who hadn't asked for anything in case it left him at a disadvantage.

'I can certainly teach you but it will take a bit of time,' Alissa controlled her voice carefully too. He had never asked her for anything before, never asked her to do anything. In fact, he rarely revealed any interest in her opinion. The only things she knew about his feelings for her, she had learned for Kieran.

'I'd like to try,' he pronounced, standing with his knees locked and a stubborn look on his face.

'Right then.' Alissa pulled herself out of the water and reached for a towel, giving her hair a quick rub and draping the towel round her neck. 'We'll go back to the deep end.'

As they passed Sally, Alissa bent down to speak to her again. 'Don't forget. Stay right here, Tulip.'

Sally giggled and nodded her head, her curls bouncing about.

'A tulip is a flower with a big fat head,' James said scornfully and Sally's face fell.

'A tulip is a flower with a beautiful head,' Alissa corrected crossly as she turned to look at him. 'You've just asked me to teach you something that has nothing to do with regular lessons. It's a favour from me to you. I don't particularly care for people who are either rude or mean, especially when they're being unpleasant to someone younger and weaker.'

James went very red and looked down at his feet. 'I'm sorry,' he muttered but it would not do for Alissa.

'You didn't insult me, James. You were being mean to Sally.'

He lifted his head and looked across at his small sister and Alissa was very pleased to see a quick compassion on his face. 'I'm sorry, Sally,' he said clearly.

'You should now say "That's all right" to James,' Alissa reminded Sally. 'Nobody can do more than apologise.'

'That's all right, James,' Sally chimed up. 'I don't mind having a big fat head if it's beautiful.'

James stiffened and Alissa gave him a playful nudge as she grinned down at him. 'Let it go,' she advised. 'Girls can be difficult. You'll get the knack of handling them.'

'Are you a girl?' James asked with the same dry air about him that spoke of Kieran.

'Only in my imagination,' Alissa told him. 'But I've still got all the tricks of the trade. Now, let's get on,' she continued briskly. 'First of all, rules. You are not to try diving when I'm not with you until I tell you that you're perfect. Second, you must not dive at the shallow end because it's dangerous.'

'Will it be dangerous for me at the deep end?' James seemed a little anxious now and looked at the water dubiously.

'Certainly not,' Alissa assured him in a very calm voice. 'You're an excellent swimmer. I wouldn't dream of letting Sally try this for years, not until she can swim as well as you and I.'

James seemed to grow a foot taller and Alissa felt a great wave of satisfaction sweep over her. She was getting close to this little boy and he needed someone to be close, someone warm and caring. Kieran cared but it was not at all the same. He needed a mother and until he got one she would have to do her best.

'Stand at the edge,' she ordered, 'and we'll do it together

first of all. We're going to fall in easily.'

'You didn't fall in,' James stated with a certain amount of indignation. 'You went in neatly with no splashes. It was smooth like…like…'

'Like a knife through butter? Possibly it was but I've been doing it for years. This is your first go. Everything takes practise. Start small, get big.'

After the second go, James was grinning as he climbed out.

'I went right to the bottom,' he said with great importance.

'I know. I was going to call out the coastguard.'

James looked at her steadily, the smile dying on his face. 'You're telling me a lie.' He had the frigid air about him that Alissa had hoped was going.

'I was joking,' Alissa corrected. 'There's a lot of difference between a joke and a lie. If there were nothing to joke about, life would be very dull. Think how funny it would have been if two great big coastguards had dived in to get you when you were perfectly safe.'

A little smile edged his lips that grew into a wide grin as he thought of the picture she painted. They went back to their starting position and James suddenly said, 'What's a lie then?'

'A lie is when you avoid telling the truth, when you turn it round for your own selfish advantage, or when you've done something that's too unpleasant for other people to know about and you have to cover it up. The trick is never to do or say anything that you're ashamed of and, if by chance you do, then own up at once and say sorry.'

James nodded and prepared for another fall into the water. 'Mummy used to lie,' he said as he fell neatly from the side.

Alissa was so shocked that she made no move to follow him. When she looked up, she saw Kieran watching them from the balcony of his room. She had no idea how long he had been there but there was a look on his face that told her he had probably been there a long time.

Alissa glared up at him. If he went around telling James that his mother was a liar, what did he expect it to do to a small child? She felt cross enough to climb up the vines and toss him into the pool. Her feelings showed on her face as usual and Kieran looked at her sardonically, his dark brows raised and then he turned away, going back into his room and leaving her with the children and her temper.

She called him to order that night at dinner. It had been simmering in her head for the rest of the afternoon and this time she made no attempt to dress for any soothing effect. She wore tight silk trousers and a flowing silky top. She marched down to dinner in her high-heeled silver sandals and faced him with more than schoolroom severity.

'I imagine you heard the little exchange with James this afternoon?' She looked sharply accusing.

'I heard more than one exchange,' he murmured, his glance running over her rather bristling beauty. 'I was an observer from the time Sally left the water. I observed James unbend sufficiently to ask a favour. I heard the lesson in good manners and gracious behaviour. I noted your safety rules with some relief and I heard your joke and the aftermath of that. Oh yes,' he added with the usual derisive air about him, 'and I applauded your graceful diving but I kept the applause silent so as not to embarrass you.'

'I'm not really interested in your appreciation of my diving skills,' Alissa told him crossly, her face flushing at the amused mockery in his glittering eyes. 'It's the *aftermath* of the joke that concerns me.'

'I fail to see why it should. You're certainly closer to James than you were originally. Don't expect to get too close however. James remembers his mother only too well and he's not likely to let any woman get close to him again, especially one who considers herself to be a girl.'

'Only in my imagination and, even then, only in my wildest moments,' Alissa glared at him with eyes as dark as night and as hard as stone. 'To hear you speak like that is appalling. You knew the woman. I refuse to believe that there isn't some softness you could tell him about her, something to prove that she's not all bad.'

The mockery died out of his eyes and she was faced with the hard glint of steel.

'I have tried to talk to my son. On the subject of his mother, however, his memory of the past has proved to be a formidable obstacle. She was without softness and she was all bad. Having lectured James on the subject of truth, do you wish to suggest that I now start lying to him?'

'She *can't* have been all bad,' Alissa snapped with frustration as she rose from the table. 'Nobody is *all* bad.'

'Believe me – *I know her*. In fact, I very soon discovered that she hadn't an ounce of warmth and gentleness in her.'

'How can you be *so* sure…*so* certain that they would be better off without her?' Alissa demanded with an angry shake of her head as she began walking towards the door.

He was on his feet and grasping hold of her arms before she'd managed to take more than a few steps.

'Believe me – I will do *anything* to look after and protect my children,' he told her, his voice heavy with menace. 'Give me one reason to suppose that you sympathise with Cynthia and…'

'And *what*…?' Alissa forced herself to stare him straight in the eye and tried to ignore the rush of fear that swept over her.

Despite her defiance, his biting rage seemed to ease almost

as swiftly as it had appeared. His powerful hands on her arms relaxed but not enough for her to escape.

'Oh, I can think of quite legal things that could happen to you,' he assured her in a taunting voice. 'The flesh can very quickly become willing.'

She gasped in outrage that was more than a little tinged with both fear and excitement.

He saw it in her eyes as swiftly as the feeling came into her head. 'But then again,' he finished, letting her go and turning back to his meal, 'I really feel that I've made enough sacrifices in my life already. I wouldn't like to be landed with you in any capacity at all, not even as a temporary mistress.'

'Come anywhere near me and you'll find out that I'm better described as a temporary assassin,' Alissa managed through stiff lips.

He gave a really amused laugh and sat down to eat. 'Shall I bring your meal up on a tray?' His voice soothed like a hunting tiger. Alissa didn't answer. She walked out of the room and deliberately slammed the door.

Much later, Alissa regretted her impulsive actions. She regretted both the words, the interference, and the way she had walked out and left her meal again.

The main reason for this regret, she had to admit, was hunger. It had taken her a good while to settle down because she had walked out on Kieran with very mixed feelings, her rage somewhat tempered by other more insidious emotions – shock, excitement and a fearful tinge of yearning.

There had been no possible way of simply going to bed. She had been much too keyed up for that and the more she waited, paced her room, watched the volcano from her balcony and muttered to herself things she might have said if she had thought of them soon enough, the more hungry she became.

By the time twelve o'clock came around, she would have given anything for a good-sized ham sandwich and a cup of tea. The appetising picture, once in her mind, was impossible to dismiss and after a while of considering the alternative – a sleepless night owing to pangs of hunger – she donned her silky robe and ventured out of her room.

The rest of the absolutely silent household was obviously fast asleep. Alissa breathed a satisfied sigh of relief and crept down the rather grand staircase that led to the hall. From there it was easy to reach the kitchen with no noise and she sped along silently, the thought of food uppermost in her mind.

There was no ham for sandwiches but there was cheese and a loaf of the delicious local bread. Alissa put the kettle on for her tea, made herself a hefty sandwich and sank her teeth into it. Heavenly!

She hummed a little tune and danced her way to the cupboard that held the cups, the sandwich waving in one hand and her other arm stretched out in time to the music in her head. She turned the tune into a waltz and did a couple of turns round the huge table in the kitchen as she waited for the kettle to boil.

Finishing off the last steps of the waltz on the return to the kettle, she twirled gracefully, watching her robe spin out around her. In her mind she was attending a rather grand ball with a dark, handsome man who just happened to have Kieran's face. She grinned around the sandwich, she could live with that, so long as he wasn't real.

A movement caught her eye and she looked up. Kieran watched her in astonishment as he lounged in the open doorway of the kitchen. He had obviously not been to bed either. He was still wearing the dark trousers and white shirt he had on at dinner.

He leaned against the side of the door as he watched her in amazement and Alissa's euphoria collapsed like a spent balloon.

If she had been on laughing terms with him it would have been much better. But as it was, with their last meeting fraught with antagonism, her last actions towards him haughty and threatening, this particular meeting quite stopped her breath.

The sandwich, which she had popped into her mouth to allow her hands to float about more gracefully, was even now clenched between her teeth. She felt like a dog, caught in the act of stealing a good, meaty bone. She felt ridiculous.

Her cheeks flushed painfully before she collected her wits and took the sandwich back into her hand. His steady, piercing grey eyes, wide and interested, made her struggle to find her voice.

'I... er... was making a sandwich,' she explained uneasily, gulping down the food in her mouth. 'The kettle hadn't boiled.'

He nodded his head slowly with excruciating politeness but said nothing at all.

'It's boiled now,' Alissa pointed out nervously. 'I can make some tea for myself before...before I go back to bed.'

He just nodded again and she wondered if he thought she was deranged. He was probably humouring her before he rushed out and phoned hastily for a replacement. Her face burned and she tore her gaze away from his and looked in despair at the kettle.

She couldn't really think of anything else to do. The picture of her bizarre conduct was far too strong in her mind for her hands to cope with kettle, teapot and cup. When she lifted the kettle, her hands shook and she had to put it down.

Another hand took over and Kieran's hands were steady

and reliable as he poured the water into the teapot, put the lid on and replaced the kettle on its stand.

She had never heard him move but he was there, right beside her, and she didn't know what to do to get herself out of this predicament.

'Thank you.' She had meant to speak firmly but it came out as little more than a whisper. He made it worse by not answering and Alissa made her cup of tea, her hands still shaking a little. She lifted the cup and saucer and turned to go but all the way she was spilling the tea and when she came level with the table, she had to put the cup and saucer down to take a firmer grip on herself.

She cast a nervous look at Kieran who was leaning against the cooker, his arms folded, one leg crossed elegantly over the other and his eyes intently on her face. Alissa knew she would say something foolish if she opened her mouth and all she could do was bite anxiously at her lower lip.

He suddenly began to laugh, warm amused laughter, quite loud and Alissa couldn't believe it. She stared at him help-lessly, her dark eyes looking too big for her face.

'Bring the cup back, pour it out and start again,' he suggested with a wide grin, 'unless you intend to lap the tea up out of the saucer. If you're going to do that, do it here. I want to watch, please. You've made me realise what I've been missing for years. Obviously I really need good enter-tainment.'

Alissa turned back to the sink with what had now become her burden. She kept her head down and when she had poured the offending liquid out, Kieran reached across and tilted her reluctant face to the light. He was still looking greatly amused and his eyes ran over her face pausing at her stub-born lips.

'Remember this the next time you feel like storming off

and leaving me at dinner,' he said with a mocking smile. 'Because the next time, I'll be waiting for my midnight cabaret!'

His head bent swiftly and his lips closed over hers with more gentleness than she expected from such a hard, ruthless man. His mouth lingered over hers before he lifted his head and licked his lips.

'Hmm! Cheese,' he murmured appreciatively. 'We must do this again. I feel quite hungry myself.'

Alissa came to startled life. The innuendo was very obvious and so far she hadn't done one thing to extricate herself from his arms. She sprang away like a startled cat and made hastily for the door.

He called after her in the same quiet, mocking voice, 'What about your tea?'

But Alissa was in the process of flying upstairs to her room – and safety. It was a long time since anyone had made her legs go weak. In fact, despite doing some frantic calculations, she couldn't remember ever feeling quite like that before in her life.

She rushed into her room and sat down with a thump on the edge of the bed, her hands against her hot cheeks as she tried to work out exactly what had happened. She hadn't even begun to sort her mind out when the door opened and Kieran walked in carrying the cup of tea.

'Milk but no sugar,' he announced, showing that his normal indifference hid a good deal of watchfulness.

'You…you didn't knock,' Alissa stated shakily.

'Does that mean I can come in regularly, provided that I knock first?'

He looked mockingly hopeful. Alissa stared at him in horror and he smiled slightly as he put the tea on her small central table.

'Drink your tea, you little battle-axe,' he advised softly.

Alissa stood on shaking legs and drew herself up to her full height as she tried belatedly to take control of the situation.

'I am not a little battle-axe!'

'No?' His eyes ran over her slender figure in the silken robe. 'I'll change that remark then. Drink your tea, you *beautiful* battle-axe…and go to sleep. You'll need all your wits about you tomorrow because you're going to be left in charge. I'm going away.'

'Oh!' Alissa's haughty posture collapsed. 'Why? Where? You didn't tell me.'

'I'm telling you now. I had intended to tell you at dinner but if you recall, you stormed out of the room.'

'How…how long…' She was looking at him with growing anxiety and his dark brows lifted in surprise.

'I really don't know. For as long as it takes, I imagine. Are you about to tell me you can't cope?'

'I can cope with anything,' Alissa stated and earned herself another glance of derision.

'With a few exceptions.' The mockery died on his face and he looked at her seriously. 'I don't expect any sort of trouble, but be alert all the same and don't go too far away from the house. If you want to go to the village nearby, take one of the men with you.'

'Who? The gardener? Or do you mean the man who simply hangs around the boat? I don't know them. I do know though that the gardener doesn't really understand what he's doing and the man by the boat spends more time throwing pebbles into the sea than anything else.'

'They work for me. Full marks for looking at them with suspicion, but don't worry about them. I know what they're doing.'

'They're your bodyguards,' Alissa surmised in a darkly dramatic voice.

Kieran smiled at her again.

'I can take care of myself, believe me. They're guarding the house, the children and you.'

'Me?' Alissa couldn't mask her astonishment.

'Naturally. You're very important in this affair. I knew I would have to leave here from time to time. I can't stay and guard you myself.'

'Are we any further forward?'

He gave a tilted smile, the mockery back in full force. 'Would you care to elaborate?'

She looked hastily away from the penetrating gaze of the silvery eyes. 'You know what I mean,' she protested as renewed heat came to her cheeks. 'I'm speaking about the kidnapping danger.'

'We're getting there. Money talks. It also opens mouths.' He turned to the door and threw his final remark over his shoulder at her. 'Don't worry, Alissa. Everything is fine and I'm very pleased with you.'

'I'm getting to know James,' she offered rather proudly.

He stopped with his hand on the door and shot her another of his lightning glances.

'I can see that. I was thinking though of your – potential.'

He walked out and closed the door silently, leaving her stunned. What did he mean? She hastily gulped her tea. It was nearly cold now but she finished it off and then almost rushed into bed. She didn't think about going across to study the volcano. The night had been explosive enough as it was.

She ran her tongue experimentally around her lips, searching for the taste of him and quickly put her head under the covers. Madwoman was right. She didn't like Kieran Tempest, so what was she doing letting him get away with

such disgraceful behaviour. Tomorrow she would sort it all
out. She would plan her moves and not leave herself so
vulnerable again.

But in the morning Kieran had gone. He must have left
very early because as she was sitting down to her breakfast,
Alissa heard the boat and seconds later she saw it cruise back
to the landing stage. He had sent it back, so she assumed he
had gone quite far afield and flown off from the airfield
where they had landed when they first came here.

He'd probably gone back to London. She tried to work out
how long the flight would be and when he would be back but
when she decided it would be a long time before she saw him
again, she put the matter firmly out of her head. She didn't
like the feeling that the house was empty without him.

So she was on her own. There were the two men outside
but she would have to be the one to watch and, even now,
she wasn't exactly sure what she was watching for.

Alissa sighed and decided she would have to make the best
of it but she wished Kieran were here. It was safe when he
was here, at least, from any outside threat.

Carl Henderson sauntered along Regent Street. He felt on top
of the world because he had a good-sized advance in his
wallet. He had more money hidden in his flat. He didn't
believe in banks because money in banks left a paper trail
that invited snoopers like the Inland Revenue. More alarming
than that, it invited interest from Kieran Tempest.

He wasn't sure how much power Tempest had but he knew
that nobody was to be trusted. For all he knew, somebody
like Tempest could waltz into a bank and inspect the books.
Tempest had known all about Bloomdale's business,
hadn't he?

No, a sock under the mattress was safer, not that a sock

would have held his fat advance. In fact, he was thinking of having a splurge with the money. He'd more or less decided to order a new suit, one that would take him to places like the club where he'd met Bloomdale.

Fine feathers made fine birds and he would be a fine bird himself now he was on the way up. No more skulking about. He would be the boss and hire others to do the dirty work in future.

In the morning sunshine he felt good.

Two men followed about thirty paces behind, well-dressed athletic looking men. They looked like police but they weren't, at least, they weren't now.

'Shall we pick him up?'

The older one shook his head as took out his mobile phone.

'No, that's not how it works. Watch and learn Sonny Boy.' He spoke on the phone. 'We've spotted him. Regent Street. Just a minute, he's going into that Italian restaurant. OK. We'll see you there.'

As Carl entered the restaurant, they were close behind him and when he sat at a corner table they sat at one across the room.

Carl looked round with a contented sigh. Pink tablecloths, candles even when it wasn't dark. A lot of greenery tastefully arranged. It was a long time since he'd had lunch at a place like this, not since Cynthia had left Tempest and the hand-outs had dried up. He still felt angry about that. He ordered a drink, shooed the waiter away and studied the menu.

His earlier feeling of being on a high had slipped away as the memory of what he had lost surfaced. He could have handled Tempest even as a brother-in-law. He would have had the handouts as well and nobody would have known he was working both sides of the coin.

When the two men slid into the spare seats at his table he

looked up, ready to snarl at them.

'What the hell do you want here? The place is almost empty. Find your own table.'

Someone else slid into the remaining seat, making him feel trapped.

'We like this one, Carl. We've decided to buy your lunch.'

Henderson went cold as he looked into the handsome face opposite him. Silvery grey eyes pinned him, making him colder still.

'What do you want, Tempest?' he blustered.

'Words, Carl. I'll buy your lunch and you'll talk. If you do well, I'll let you go. But be advised, I already know the gist of it. All I want is your version.'

Kieran signalled for the waiter and ordered for all of them. When they had privacy, he looked at Henderson icily.

'Now, tell me a story,' he said, 'and make it good.'

Alissa kept strictly to routine, lessons and then either swimming and continuing the diving lessons for James, or a picnic on the beach with the children. The man by the boat was, if anything, more watchful and, although she appreciated the reason for this, it served to make her feel quite trapped.

Alissa asked the children if they had ever been to the village nearby and Sally couldn't remember ever going there. James said he'd been but not for a long time.

'I wouldn't mind going back to have a look,' he ventured hopefully and as far as Alissa was concerned, that settled it.

They prepared to go the next afternoon. Alissa took the children to the beach later, in order to make arrangements with the man by the boat and he looked quite startled when he realised she was about to accost him.

'Tomorrow afternoon, I'm taking the children to the village,' she informed him briskly. 'Mr Tempest wants me to have a man with me and it's either you or the gardener. I've given it some thought and it seems to me that he does more work than you, so I'm letting you accompany us.'

'Thanks, Miss Brent. Mr Tempest did mention it. He said you'd probably pick me.'

'I can't think why he…' Alissa began haughtily, but all she got was a wide grin and no sign of annoyance.

'He told me you'd been spying on the two of us and decided that I wasn't doing a damned thing. The name's Greg Snow, by the way.'

'You mean he actually speaks to you? I mean, apart from giving orders?'

'Known him a long time,' Greg Snow murmured in amusement. He was an American from his accent and he looked tough and resourceful.

'Just exactly what are you?' Alissa looked at him very seriously, inviting him to confess. 'I think you're his bodyguard but he denies it.'

'He's pretty good at guarding his own body,' Greg assured her, his grin even wider. 'I'd hesitate to tackle him without some decided advantage, like a brick wall, to hide behind.'

'Then I can't see any reason for you being here.'

'I'm an investigator.'

'What do you investigate?'

'Anything Mr Tempest thinks looks fishy, or anyone he's particularly interested in. For example,' he added, 'I investigated you.'

'There's nothing fishy about me!' Alissa looked at him indignantly.

'He already knew that. He just wanted to make sure you wouldn't become a liability. For example, I backtracked you to France. I know all about you, everything but your dress size and I imagine Mr Tempest knows that.'

'What are you implying?' Alissa stared at him in a frosty manner, her cheeks flushed with annoyance.

'Nothing ma'am. No innuendo intended. It's just that Mr Tempest has a way of knowing most things, as if he's got a through line to heaven.'

'All the same,' Alissa snapped, not altogether mollified and knowing that she looked extremely prim. 'I don't think I shall let you go with us to the village.'

'I doubt if you'll like Harry any better.' He nodded in the direction of the so-called gardener. 'He's British, but he's an ex-paratrooper and he's tough.'

'And what were you?' Alissa directed a quick anxious look at Harry who was ignoring all this but giving the definite impression of watching them out of the corner of his eye.

'Me? Oh, I'm an ex-cop. I'm good at public relations,' he assured her.

'The public must miss you terribly,' Alissa muttered sarcastically. She gave an impatient sigh. 'Very well. Come to the house at one o' clock and pick us up.'

'Yes, ma'am.'

Alissa cast a withering glance at him and left him to continue his task of simply hanging about. She wasn't sure if Greg Snow was laughing at her, in fact she rather thought he was. She also had the uneasy feeling that Kieran would have been laughing at her when he assigned his minion to escort duty. She hadn't forgotten the debacle of the cup of tea and cheese sandwich. She hadn't forgotten how it felt to have his hands and lips on her either.

'Greg is a crack shot,' James told her quite casually as they walked back to the house later.

'He's *what*?' Alissa stopped and stared at James in horror. The children had been well out of hearing distance when she'd spoken to the man. This sort of knowledge was most unsuitable for children.

'He's a crack shot,' James repeated patiently, scuffing his foot through the dry sand. 'He can shoot the skin off a rice pudding, so can Harry.'

Sally began to giggle and Alissa felt as if she'd stepped into a sort of weird wonderland. The very blasé way James spoke of such things was unbelievable.

She eyed him sternly. 'How do you know these unlikely facts?'

He gave her a satisfied little smirk. 'Dad told me. They're often with us. They do jobs for Dad.'

'I would not have thought your father had that many rice puddings for them to practice on,' Alissa said in a starchy voice, but her outrage was somewhat dispelled when James began to giggle too.

'You're really funny, Alissa,' he laughed and it made the whole day worthwhile. In fact, it made the whole trip worthwhile. James was definitely unbending fast.

Alissa took a deep breath and looked around her. She had a sudden feeling of deep contentment. This place was a real paradise. The house was glowing in the sunlight, flowered creepers on the old stone work of the walls. The curtains of her room were blowing in the soft breeze and by now she was used to the heat, although it was not at any time overwhelming.

'Let's have a quick dip in the pool before lunch,' she suggested impulsively and the children were instantly enthusiastic. Only one thing marred the perfection. She genuinely missed Kieran.

The thought drove the smile from her face. That way lay insanity. He was clever, hard, ruthless and with an unendingly bitter distrust of women. But there seemed to be a very large gap in the household now that he was gone.

Her mind went treacherously back to the way he had kissed her. Gently, a sort of tender salute as if he cared about her. She knew he didn't care at all but the idea ran around in her mind. He had been annoyed when Andy Dodds had scared her with his chilling tales of volcanoes. He seemed to be taking care of her without her even knowing it. And she was missing him badly even though her common sense advised her to employ her usual caution. Her common sense couldn't do anything at all about her wayward thoughts and dreams.

chapter seven

The following morning, Martha popped her head round the door of the schoolroom. 'There's a visitor, Miss Brent. As Mr Tempest is away, I thought you should perhaps come down to see her.'

'Her?' Alissa looked surprised.

Martha glanced at the children and then came into the room. 'Mrs Fox,' she whispered, 'the one I told you about.'

'Oh. Right. I'll be down.' Alissa glanced at the children too and then said, 'I'm just going downstairs for a minute. I'll not be long.'

Sally just nodded her curly head and didn't look up. James nodded too but not before he had fixed her with a peculiarly penetrating look that she normally associated with his father.

'Is anything wrong, James?'

'No. I'll watch Sally while you're out.' He was back to being stiff, aloof and, once again, taking shelter behind his usual air of being unapproachable. But Alissa decided to ignore it.

It had been interesting to also note Martha's attitude. She wasn't pleased about this visitor and neither was James. In all probability, James had heard everything because he didn't miss much. So now was her chance to get a good look at Mrs Fox and decide for herself.

She decided at the very first glance. Lara Fox was in her mid-thirties as far as Alissa could tell, and she was very glossy, attractive in a brittle way that spoke more of the front of a fashion magazine than any natural attractiveness. Her eyes were pale blue and her hair was dark red. The hair colour was not natural either. This knowledge gave Alissa a rather malicious burst of satisfaction that she made no attempt to curb.

The woman gave a gleaming smile but it didn't reach her eyes and her whole expression was one of calculating alertness. She didn't like competition and this obvious fact almost had Alissa smiling to herself. Had Lara Fox but known it, she was facing no competition at all, merely a disguised watchdog.

'I understand Kieran is away?' Mrs Fox summed Alissa up rapidly. 'If he'd let me know, I wouldn't have wasted my time coming over here.'

Alissa beamed at her. 'Well, I'm sorry. I expect Martha thought you had some business here and when Kieran is away, I take over.'

This remark daringly skirted the truth. He had told her she was in charge but she knew he meant just with the children. It was also audacious to call him Kieran but Alissa couldn't help the little dig, her interest in Lara Fox's reaction driving her on unwisely.

The reaction was swift and irritated. 'In charge? I thought you were the nanny or something.'

'Goodness, no! I'm a teacher and bodyguard.' Alissa kept a very straight face. She hadn't been called upon to do this sort of thing before. It was a bit like fencing and she was beginning to enjoy herself with what she readily admitted was a certain vindictive pleasure.

'A bodyguard?' The sharp blue eyes ran over Alissa as if looking for ironclad muscles. 'Who are you supposed to guard?'

'Anyone in danger,' Alissa said solemnly. 'Although,' she added with a coy smile, 'Kieran is more than capable of guarding himself and all of us. I only go into action when he's away.'

The dark colour of annoyance flooded Lara Fox's cheeks as she stood impatiently. 'Well, as he's obviously not here, I may as well go.'

Alissa tried to look hospitable. 'Will you have coffee?'

'No thank you. I didn't come for coffee. I came to see Kieran.'

'I'll let him know that you called,' Alissa promised sweetly. 'I'm surprised he didn't tell you he was going.'

'It probably slipped his mind. I'll be in touch when he gets back.'

She was definitely not going to ask when that would be and Alissa hid a gleeful smile. This was a resounding victory, although for the life of her she couldn't understand why she wanted to win.

She told herself firmly that it was because this woman was too hard-faced to be with children. If Lara Fox was going to be hanging around here in any capacity whatever, it would be bad for James especially. She looked as if the only person who would interest her deeply was herself.

Alissa's suspicious mind began to wonder how the woman had known they were here at all. The only thing she could come up with was that Kieran had telephoned her and if he had done, then he was missing this hard-as-nails creature. The thought made Alissa more annoyed than ever.

It was only as she was seeing her disgruntled guest off the premises that Alissa realised she had left the door of the room open. As they walked into the hall, she saw Martha lurking about in the shadows, quite obviously spying.

She called her to order after the car with Lara Fox aboard had shot off, accompanied by the sound of angry revving from the engine.

'Martha. Surely you weren't eavesdropping?'

'Well, as a matter-of-fact, I was,' Martha confessed, her face struggling with amusement. 'And I must say,' she finished, giving in to the urgent desire to laugh, 'I've never heard such a complete put-down done so skilfully. I don't mind admitting that I dislike that woman and heaven help the children if she ever marries Mr. Tempest.'

'He cares about his children more than anything else,' Alissa pointed out quietly. 'Whoever he marries will be chosen with that thought in mind.'

'He's a man,' Martha reminded her in a more sombre manner. 'He must get lonely sometimes. He needs somebody who cares about the children as much as he does and if he's going to marry again, that person is definitely not Mrs Fox. But she does come round here and she always has that air about her of someone who's quite close to being the mistress of the place.'

'How did she know we were all here?' Alissa muttered, suspicious again.

'She phoned yesterday. I took the call myself. I didn't tell her he would be away because I didn't know.'

Martha went away to the kitchen, shaking her head ruefully and Alissa began to climb the stairs with a thoughtful expression on her face. If Lara Fox had spoken to Kieran, then he hadn't told her he would be away. The other alternative was that she knew he was away and had come to assess the opposition.

If Kieran was really lonely, lonely enough to contemplate marriage again, then Lara Fox was the most unsuitable candidate ever. It would be tossing James back into a nightmare. However, there was nothing Alissa could do about that. Kieran didn't look as if he would take kindly to any well-meant advice.

Alissa looked up and James was there above her, his face pushed almost through the dark wood of the balustrade at the top of the stairs. Martha was not the only one who had been eavesdropping.

'If you get your head stuck in the bars, it's going to be a bit tricky to release you,' Alissa pointed out. 'I really would hate to take a saw to that old, ornate woodwork. You just might have to stay there permanently, like an ancient gargoyle.'

James gave a sheepish grin and rapidly extricated himself. He was standing waiting when Alissa made it to the top of the stairs.

'I was listening,' he confessed, looking at her as if he expected instant punishment.

'You know, I rather figured that out for myself.' She put her hand on his shoulder and shepherded him back to the schoolroom. 'I was quite at ease, knowing as I did that you were watching Sally. After all, she's quite alone.'

'She's all right. I wasn't on the stairs for long.'

'Long enough to spy on adults,' Alissa reminded him.

'Are you angry with me, Alissa?'

She glanced down at his pale little face before giving his shoulder an encouraging squeeze. 'No, I'm not angry at all. It's not a thing I would advise in future, however. Spying on people usually leads to trouble and very often you don't quite understand what you hear under these rather difficult conditions. It's very easy to get the wrong end of the stick.'

'She wants to marry Dad,' James pointed out gloomily.

'Those are merely Martha's speculations.'

'They're not. I've known for ages. She comes here often when we're over and she comes to London too. Dad takes her out. She wants to marry him. I know he'll finally give in because she's so pushy.'

There really was no answer to that and Alissa was glad when they arrived at the schoolroom and this conversation could be dropped. She could quite understand James' need to pick up information in any way he could but she was also quite sure that Kieran cared too much about his children to allow them to face life with another uncaring woman.

It might be a kindly action for Kieran to set their minds at rest, if only for James' sake.

'Don't count your chickens,' Alissa advised.

'She's more of a big red hen,' James muttered.

Sally looked up from her book. 'I saw Mrs Fox go. She looked all cross. I watched out of the window.'

'Then, goodness me,' Alissa exclaimed, 'we have a lot of time to make up. In future, I shall discourage visitors unless your father is here.'

'She left a lot more quickly when *you* saw to her.' James pointed this out with an air of satisfaction and Alissa had to make a silent acknowledgement that she too felt satisfied with her ability to dispatch the unwanted with speed.

'Let's get on,' she suggested. 'Don't forget that we're going out this afternoon. We want to go with a clear conscience, knowing that we've done plenty of work.'

Alissa was not quite sure that her own conscience was clear. In some rather surreptitious way, she seemed to have been attempting to interfere with Kieran's life. He would not be pleased if he found out and she was sure that Lara Fox would tell him at the very first opportunity.

The village was far enough away from the house to require transport and when he came for them, Greg Snow drove up in a weird-looking vehicle that was obviously a four-wheel drive. It had no sides and a roof that looked very much like a sun canopy. The children didn't bat an eye but after a glance at Alissa's open-mouth astonishment, James informed her that Greg had come for them in 'the poke'.

Alissa didn't enquire further.

At any rate, the canopy kept the hot sun from them and it was quite a pleasant vehicle to ride in. They arrived in quite some style and Alissa was able to observe the village for a good while as they approached.

By now she had grown accustomed to the rather splendid architecture of the house, the heavy stone work, the carvings and the balconies, the feeling of the grandeur of old Spain. The village too was old Spain but absolutely nothing was grand, with the possible exception of an ancient church that looked as if it had been transported from Seville.

The rest of the village was so obviously country-poor that Alissa felt uncomfortable to have driven up with money to buy things. She need not have worried. The whole place was filled with happy people who smiled at them and inspected their unusual form of transport as they pointed out the few shops.

She murmured her anxieties to Greg and he looked quite surprised.

'They're not poor, not by their standards. These people are farmers with good, rich land. Their produce goes over to the mainland each day.'

He pointed to the harbour which was at that moment a bustling place, filled with boats, all of them being loaded. 'Most families have a boat, or share one with a neighbour. I'd like to bet there's not one person here who could really be called poor. Don't let the houses fool you. In this climate, buildings rapidly disintegrate and need quite a lot of care. The people here are too busy making money on the land. In winter, they'll get round to the houses.'

'Is it ever winter?'

'Couple of weeks. They'll be out then, painting their houses and shouting to each other. They're a happy lot. They haven't yet realised that life can't go on without a television set and a washing machine.'

The children made a beeline for the small shops and later went down to the harbour to watch the boats. Alissa went along too with Greg firmly by their side. She surreptitiously looked for his gun but as far as she could tell he didn't have one, at least it wasn't visible.

'James tells me you're a crack shot,' she said casually but Greg Snow was not the sort of man to be taken by surprise. He gave her a wryly-amused look.

'It's the business I'm in.'

'I can't see your gun,' Alissa remarked with a certain amount of disappointed indignation.

His ready grin widened. 'It's strapped to my ankle. It's well within reach but it doesn't do to advertise the fact.'

'Would you use it?' Alissa couldn't keep the awed respect from her voice.

'If it became necessary. So far it hasn't been necessary at all but I'm a bodyguard after all.'

'You told me you were an investigator,' Alissa reminded him triumphantly.

'That too. I told you though, Kieran Tempest is more than capable of taking care of himself. I'm here to guard them,' he finished, nodding towards the children. 'I'm under orders to guard you too, Miss Brent.'

Alissa gave a thoughtful frown. Working out her exact duties here was becoming quite problematic. The teaching was straightforward but right from the first, Kieran had informed her that he needed her for her fierce abilities.

As far as she could see, she didn't need any fierce abilities at all. The fighting spirit could be left to Greg Snow and the silent Harry. Maybe Kieran thought she was good at spotting danger? Alissa would have made a safe bet that Greg and Harry were better with that particular skill too.

In spite of her inner musings, Alissa enjoyed the afternoon and as they drove back to the house she felt sleepily happy. Even the pulsating glow coming from El Bueno did nothing to make her uneasy. She was getting used to it, just as she was getting used to the house, the children and Kieran.

As they walked in through the open front door, Martha hurried forward and beamed at them.

'He's back.' She looked as if she had both planned and forecast Kieran's return. 'He's in his study right now but he asked me to let you know as soon as you came in that he's waiting to see the children.' She stood with her hands folded like a Victorian housekeeper.

'Right away,' Alissa promised in a stunned voice. Maybe it was the way Martha had phrased it but the whole thing sounded a little quaint to her.

Bring the children to me as soon as they return.

It made Alissa feel like a governess in some old film. She was to straighten her skirts and usher the children in to see their father. Her heart had leapt when she'd heard he was back and she had to work hard at keeping a blank expression on her face.

'Does the master wish to see me?'

Martha had no time to do anything but give her a startled glance.

'Naturally, Miss Brent,' Kieran assured her from the open door of his study. He was eyeing her with amusement and she was relieved when Sally raced across to throw herself at her father.

Alissa looked at James and he was giving her a sideways glance of understanding. His lips were twitching with amusement, just like his father's.

'You're too clever by half,' Alissa muttered and James grinned up at her.

'I've got to know you now,' he whispered. 'I know when you're being sarcastic. It's always so funny.'

'Let's hope you father thinks so,' Alissa said, driving him on in front of her.

'He does,' James stated, keeping his voice low. 'I often see him laughing at you when you're not looking.'

Once again, there was no answer to that and Alissa moved into Kieran's study with a rather pink face, James at her side, still grinning.

'Did you buy anything in the village?' Kieran asked the children and that gave Alissa a moment's respite while they told their father about the trip and showed him the small useless objects they had gathered *en route*.

Alissa watched in silence, her dark eyes running from one to the other. The children were happy, very much changed from the subdued attitude they had arrived with weeks ago. James had obviously blossomed. She smiled with satisfaction and when she looked up, Kieran was watching her, the piercing grey eyes more softened than she could ever have hoped to see.

'I brought you some snorkelling equipment,' he told James, handing out a mask and goggles. 'Only to be used when Alissa is with you, of course. I've been watching your progress with the diving lessons and this is a reward.'

James was obviously thrilled and Sally looked on expectantly as Kieran opened another parcel. It was a little bikini with a frilly skirt and a big sun hat to match. Sally was delighted but her face fell when she waited for him to produce another parcel. 'What about Lissa? Have you left her out?'

'Of course not,' Kieran said. 'I brought her a bikini like yours.'

Sally beamed and Alissa felt heat flooding into her face.

'We can wear them tomorrow,' Sally announced excitedly, and Kieran watched Alissa's flushed cheeks with amused interest.

'I'm sure your father is joking,' Alissa said firmly. 'When somebody goes away they just bring presents for children. Now would you both like to go and get ready for your meal?'

She knew she was really acting like an old-fashioned governess now and hoped James wasn't noticing. He was too busy inspecting his new equipment and Alissa hurried them out into the hall and up the stairs as soon as she could pry Sally from Kieran, who was being smothered in kisses and looking more amused by the second.

Alissa managed to keep out of his way until dinnertime but with the children safely in bed she had to go down and face those cool, grey eyes. She was dreading it because she'd suddenly realised just how pleased and excited she was about Kieran's return. She felt as if a growing sadness had lifted and the feeling was totally unexpected.

She was *glad* he was back and clearly that reaction on her part wouldn't do at all. She had no intention of becoming any closer to him than she was already and, besides, he might know about Lara Fox's visit. She had no idea how much he talked to Martha.

If he was annoyed about her little interview with Mrs Fox, she would have to try and keep her temper. She really didn't want to quarrel with him on his first night back.

He was waiting for her in the small drawing room and as soon as she walked in, he turned and poured her a drink without asking what she wanted. Even that startled Alissa. Already her place appeared to be so well established in this small family, that he seemed to know what she liked without asking. An involvement that she had never intended to happen.

'Any problems while I've been away?' Kieran asked, handing her the drink.

Naturally, Lara Fox sprang to mind immediately. 'No. Everything was normal,' she told him firmly. 'We've only had the one excursion to the village and that was this afternoon. Greg Snow went with us.'

'I know,' Kieran said, his eyes on her face. 'I had a word with Greg when you went up to see to the children. I also had a little goodnight chat with James. Greg informed me about your trip. He told me you kept him on his toes and looked slightly sceptical about his ability to defend you in times of trouble.'

'I'll scream for him if I need him,' Alissa muttered, looking intently into her drink to avoid the eyes that seemed to be able to see right through her.

'You can scream for me if you need help. Then there's James of course. You seem to have captured his heart. According to my son, you're the most amusing woman in the whole world.'

Alissa's skin heated yet again. The only thing that sprang into her mind was the remark that James had made about her skill in dispatching Lara Fox. She decided to get her story in quickly and head off trouble before it became a major problem.

She summoned up a casual voice. 'Oh, I almost forgot to tell you, Mrs Fox came. She was only here for a few minutes. In fact, she didn't even stay for coffee.'

'How disappointing for you,' Kieran murmured. 'There are no visitors here and Lara would make quite a good friend for you when you're feeling lonely.'

'I don't ever feel lonely,' Alissa assured him strongly, looking up into the searching eyes. Annoyance flared in her voice. 'I like it here and…and, anyway, I'm busy with the children most of the time.' She would rather have been offered a pet rattlesnake than make a friend of Lara Fox.

'Very good,' Kieran drawled. 'That sets my mind at rest. I was a little worried that you might find things boring while I was away.'

'I…I had too much to do,' Alissa assured him uneasily, wondering if he was any good at reading minds and searching out forbidden thoughts.

They went in to dinner and Alissa was glad to get on with her meal and put an end to this rather worrying conversation.

Kieran also ate his meal and said nothing at all. He was too busy thinking about Alissa. God, he'd missed her. It was almost impossible to realise just how much he'd wanted her with him. For once, his mind had not been concentrated solely on the pursuit of his plans.

He'd spent some uncomfortable nights thinking about her. He remembered how she trembled when he kissed her, how she felt when he held her close and how she had forgotten to move away. His body had registered every curve of hers and he had carried the memory with him ever since.

She was tall, slender and fierce as a dragon, but she had been no dragon then. She had been soft and docile, swaying into him, yielding. There was a great well of love inside her that she hid behind her sharp and aggressive attitude to life. And he trusted her completely.

Alissa felt too worked up to simply sit in total silence. 'Did you do what you wanted to do?'

'I didn't want to do anything. I had to go. Had I been following my own inclinations, I would have stayed right here.'

'I expect business called too strongly,' Alissa murmured.

'Duty called. My people had managed to track down my ex-brother-in-law.'

Alissa's head shot up. 'The one who tried to take the children?'

'The very same. I suppose I should keep you up to date as that's the reason you're here.'

'Have you had him arrested?' Alissa stared at him urgently.

'No. I'd rather have him free.' His eyes roamed over her face, lingering for a few seconds on her parted lips. 'I'm giving him plenty of rope at the moment. Having found him, we won't lose him again. From now on, I'll know every move he makes. I'll be informed of each breath he takes. I'll also know who his friends and acquaintances are. We can pick him up at any time we choose, but I want the children to be safe from now on. Permanently safe.'

'Is it possible with you being so wealthy? It seems to me that everyone spies on you. They do it all the time. Maybe someone else will eventually get the idea of kidnapping the children.'

'I'm just a businessman.'

'You're a financial genius,' Alissa corrected. 'That makes you vulnerable.'

'The children make me vulnerable and we can't stay here all the time.'

'Then some plan will have to be worked out so that they're safe wherever they are. You're not the only wealthy man in the world and you seem to have plenty of guards around you. The children will need to go to school, to live a normal life.'

'As far as I know, there was no problem at all before this attempt in London,' Kieran said tight-lipped. 'When I've got everyone boxed in, there may well be nothing further. This whole thing has made me suspicious. Only James saw his Uncle Carl.'

'If James said it was his uncle, then it was,' Alissa stated. 'James is very clever. He thinks deeply.'

'Obviously,' Kieran murmured with a sudden return to wry humour. 'At the moment he appears to be thinking of you more than anyone else. Apparently, he admires your diving skills, your sharp tongue and your ability to dispatch unwanted guests with incredible speed.'

'If you mean Mrs Fox,' Alissa challenged, 'she refused to stay.'

'I know. James doesn't seem to have missed much.'

'I remonstrated with him on the subject of eavesdropping.'

'How else is he to find things out?' Kieran taunted. 'With you around, the desire to listen in on conversations is over-whelming. I often have the urge to do it myself.'

'If we're going to quarrel it would be best if I left the room,' Alissa snapped.

'Fine. I'll come up to your bedroom to give you your present.' Kieran was watching her intently again, a smile edging his lips. He found her delightful, the only woman he had ever felt delighted with. He wondered what she would do if he walked across and kissed her now?

Before she could say anything, he drew a long leather case from his pocket and put it on the table in front of her. She didn't know what to say. She just stared at it and he gave an exaggerated sigh as he flipped the case open and a row of glittering stones almost dazzled her.

It was a bracelet and Alissa had no idea whether it was real or not. It was just beautiful.

'I…I can't accept this.' She didn't look up but he stood and came round to her, taking the bracelet from the case and fastening it round her wrist as she sat there in awe.

'Why not? You deserve rewards. I must think highly of you or I wouldn't be paying you double salary. You're a very entertaining person too and this place is so quiet.'

'I don't know what to say.'

'Thank you?' He suggested this with an amused look at her stunned expression. 'I seriously considered the bikini but perhaps the bracelet is a better choice. After all, I was able to put the bracelet on for you…'

He just left the statement hanging in the air, the implication unsaid and Alissa felt suddenly very breathless.

'Speaking of salary,' he finished when she was utterly incapable of speech, 'so far, I haven't paid you. It's very remiss of me. Tomorrow I'll make out a cheque for you to bring us up-to- date.'

'It…it's all right,' Alissa stammered. 'I trust you.'

'Not too much, I hope,' he advised and Martha walked in at the best possible moment to announce that coffee was served in the drawing room.

Alissa was trembling and she didn't want to face him in there all by herself. 'I think I'll pass on the coffee,' she said as Martha left the room.

'A good idea,' Kieran taunted. 'I'll see you at midnight then when you come down for your tea and sandwich. Don't start the cabaret until I'm there will you? It seems such a long time since we had our night-time entertainment. While I've been away, I've been suffering painful withdrawal symptoms.'

'Please don't,' Alissa whispered anxiously. He was making her feel funny inside, shaky and breathless.

'Not until you stop being afraid of me,' he promised. He stood and came to escort her to the door, his eyes not leaving hers but she couldn't allow him to get close.

'Goodnight,' she said quickly, backing away and he

stopped perfectly still and smiled into her frantic eyes.

'If you like, Alissa,' he agreed.

Alissa just fled. There was no other way to describe her hasty retreat to her room and Kieran didn't leave the hall until she was out of sight. She couldn't actually hear him laughing but she had a good imagination. She was also remembering that on the occasion in question, he had kissed her, even though it had been in a very mocking way. She closed her door firmly and then sat down to look at the bracelet.

It really was very beautiful. Composed of delicate blue and white stones set in gold, Alissa could only stare bemusedly at the bracelet, hoping that they were not precious stones. Real sapphires and diamonds would have cost a small fortune, far more than she could ever imagine earning on a teacher's salary.

That was when she remembered the long case it had been in. She had rushed out and left it behind and she would have to go down and get it, or Kieran would think she was an ungrateful wretch. With any luck, it would still be on the table in the dining room.

Alissa went down stealthily, hoping she would not encounter Kieran at all. Martha was still clearing away and when Alissa came into the room she looked quite surprised.

'I left a long leather case here,' Alissa told her.

Martha smiled and nodded. 'I just this minute gave it to Mr Tempest. I thought it might be his. He's got it in the small drawing room. He's still having his coffee.'

There was no real alternative. Alissa had to face him again and with Martha watching she couldn't even put it off until morning. She went to the door of the drawing room and took a deep breath before walking in. She needed the deep breath because she was instantly pinned to the spot by the gleam in his grey eyes.

'You've either changed your mind about the coffee or you've remembered the jewellery case.'

'I remembered the case. I left it on the table in the dining room and when I got upstairs I...' Alissa stopped and then looked at him a little frantically. 'Please tell me that this bracelet isn't real?' she asked anxiously.

The grey eyes narrowed and swept over her face. 'It is real. Why should that bother you?'

'Because I'm not used to things like this. It's too much. I really can't accept it.'

She began to unfasten it and at the sign of her very real agitation, Kieran stood and came towards her.

'I wanted to buy it for you, Alissa. I can assure that it wasn't outrageously expensive.'

'It is to me,' she assured him, still trying to find the way to loosen the catch.

By then he was right in front of her and his hand covered hers, stopping any further attempts to remove the bracelet. 'Alissa, I'm very rich. This is merely a little present.'

'But I don't need a present.' She looked up at him uneasily and his eyes captured hers at once.

'I needed to buy it for you,' he said in the same soft voice. 'I found to my astonishment that I missed you when I was away.' He lifted his hand and let his fingers trail warmly over her flushed cheeks. 'Just tell me you missed me too, and we'll call it even.'

Alissa didn't know what to say. She knew perfectly well that she'd missed him but telling him would seem excessive. He was constantly battling with her, constantly taunting. She just went on staring up into his eyes and he gave a small, greatly exaggerated sigh.

'Then I'll have to find out for myself.' His hand curled round her face. Alissa felt his lips brush hers gently and then close firmly over her mouth when she made no move to pull free.

In fact, she didn't feel like pulling free at all. It was a wonderful feeling, dreamy, warm and she had an urgent desire to move closer and wind her arms round his neck. It was only by exerting a great effort that she stayed where she was, and when Kieran lifted his head and looked down at her he was smiling.

'You,' he said quietly, 'are going to fight me to the last breath. You don't give in to your feelings unless the feeling is one of resistance, do you?'

She just stared up at him as she had been doing all the time and his smile widened. He ran his fingers through her hair, in a gesture of possession.

Alissa almost leapt away from him. 'Is…is this why you bought me the bracelet?' she asked shakily. 'Is it so that…'

'So that you'll sleep with me? I already told you why I bought it. You're being pampered. Hasn't that ever happened to you before? Is it only your sister and brother-in-law who want to spoil you? Surely some man has looked at your beautiful dark eyes and your long pale hair and wondered why you feel the need to fight all the time?'

'I take care of myself.'

'You don't need to while I'm here. I want to protect you and I've decided to be very indulgent with you.'

'I won't…If you imagine for one minute that I'll…'

'I haven't asked you, Alissa,' he reminded her in an amused voice. 'Maybe the next time we meet at midnight for tea and dancing, I'll get around to it then.'

'I won't keep the bracelet,' Alissa stated as her face flamed with embarrassment and forbidden excitement.

Kieran just laughed, then went back to his coffee as if nothing had happened at all and after another couple of seconds of struggle with the bracelet, Alissa fled yet again.

She couldn't seem to remove the bracelet, despite her determined and increasingly frantic attempts to do so.

Next morning, she awoke with a deep indentation in her arm where the bracelet had risen to its maximum width and pressed into her arm as she slept. She was still wearing it when she went down to breakfast and as soon as she walked in, Kieran's eyes went straight to it.

He gave one of his special frowns and came round to her at once, his fingers slickly removing the bracelet and then dropping it by her plate as if it were a cheap imitation.

'It has a hidden catch,' he said. 'I'm sorry. It must have been uncomfortable.'

Sally was watching the bracelet with glowing eyes, but the eyes that were worrying Alissa were definitely masculine ones – James and Kieran.

James was doing a little of his own summing up, his glance switching from the bracelet, to Alissa and then to his father. His eyes came back to her face, resting there thoughtfully and Alissa had a very hard time trying to look nonchalant and normal.

Kieran was also watching her, but this morning there was none of the usual mockery in his eyes. Like his son, he seemed to be quietly deliberating, weighing things up in his mind and Alissa found it was impossible to make any sort of conversation at all.

'Can they take a day off today, do you think?' Kieran's sudden question caused Alissa to glance up at him in surprise.

'If you like,' she agreed. 'They both worked hard while you were away.'

'Then shall we have the day together? I've asked Dodds to fly us all up to the volcano and this afternoon we can sit around the pool while you try out your new equipment.' He glanced at the children.

His suggestion went down very well and, some time later, as the children raced off to get ready for this day of unexpected treats, Alissa stayed behind and summoned up the courage to face Kieran.

'I want to give you the bracelet back,' she told him.

'Don't,' he said softly. 'You really earned it and I'm not joking now. You've done much more than teach the children, Alissa. You've achieved more with James in the few weeks you've been here than I've been able to achieve in the last three years. I honestly believe he's coming out of it all. He's happy and he never stops talking about you. You're his friend. He finds you warm and safe.'

'I'm not a very warm person,' Alissa began and he smiled in his usual mysterious way.

'Then you don't know yourself very well. You've brought a lot of feminine warmth into our lives. Even Martha feels the need to be constantly pointing out your good qualities.'

'I don't need to be rewarded. I'm getting well-paid.'

'Double the salary, I know.' He grinned across at her. 'Let's just say that the bracelet is for the extras. And I really will not try to seduce you,' he added when her eyes opened widely and suspiciously. 'Now what about the trip to El Bueno?' He asked this crisply, in a voice that told her the other discussion was definitely over. 'Do you think you dare risk it?'

'Are the children really going?'

'They are. In half an hour, our expert is going to arrive in his helicopter and take us for a spin.'

'I expect he knows what he's doing,' Alissa muttered.

'You don't have to go,' he assured her but she looked up quickly, her lips set in a stubborn way he had already become accustomed to.

'I do. If the children are going, then so am I. I wouldn't forgive myself if anything happened to them. If something is going to happen, then it can happen to me too.'

Kieran's eyes narrowed and glowed like crystal, the morning sun catching their brilliant gleam. He regarded her seriously for a long time.

'Do they mean so much to you?'

She looked up at him with an air of defiance about her. 'Yes, they do.'

'Then we'll all go together,' Kieran stated.

'I hope that's not a dark prediction,' Alissa muttered as she left the table and went to get ready.

This time she could hear him laughing even when she was going upstairs and it reminded her of her thoughts about him when she had first seen him. Then, she had never imagined he would be able to laugh. Maybe she had earned the bracelet after all if she had managed that.

In any case, getting him to take it back seemed beyond her powers of persuasion. Her cheeks grew hot and she dived into her room when she saw James coming along the corridor, watching her with that little calculating glance that had made her feel awkward at the table earlier. His very grown-up attitude to life was due, no doubt, to the time he'd spent with his father, and also probably to the alarmingly clever Tempest intellect.

She wasn't at all sure whether James was her champion – or a small watchdog intent on keeping life exactly as he wanted it to be.

chapter eight

Alissa was only just ready when she heard the sound of a helicopter overhead. As she looked from her window, it landed neatly on the lawn at the front of the house and Andy Dodds climbed out, grinning up at her as she stood on her balcony.

'Going to risk it then?' he shouted and she nodded uneasily before diving back into her room.

She had decided to wear shorts and had advised Sally to do the same thing. She didn't know if it was wise. For all she knew, it would be cold in a helicopter. Still, Andy surely wouldn't keep the doors open. If he did, she would scream like a banshee.

They were waiting for her when she went down to the hall and the shorts seemed to have been a very bad idea when she saw Kieran's eyes roam over the length of her legs. Andy Dodds was doing the same thing but he didn't worry her at all. When Kieran looked at her she felt faint, her heartbeats thundering in her ears. There was enough worrying her already without facing anything else.

'Can I sit in the front with the pilot?' James pulled at his father's hand and Kieran looked at him with surprise.

'Of course. Why not? I have to guard the women. You can ask the questions.'

The remarks seemed to please everyone. James looked very self-important and Sally beamed at this compliment.

Alissa felt sick with fright.

'You can back out now if you want to,' Kieran said as the children ran ahead with Andy Dodds.

'No thank you. I'll come. I want to be with the children.'

'Well, I'll sit in the back with you, just in case you want to be with me too.'

She looked up at him quickly, an expression of distress on her face.

'Please don't start a fight until we get back. I've had to gear myself up for this and I need every ounce of courage for myself. I've never been in a helicopter before and it looks too flimsy for flying over the volcano. Then again, there's the volcano itself. I keep thinking it will pull us down and it must be hot in there. I haven't forgotten about the molten lava and the way it can simply explode.'

'Oh, Alissa,' Kieran murmured. 'There really is no need for you to face this. I honestly thought you would refuse to come. We can easily go without you.'

'No,' she said stubbornly.

Kieran gave a resigned sigh and walked quietly beside her with no further words.

'One order only,' he told Andy as they came to the helicopter. 'Fly us up and round but not directly across the top. We'll look from the edge.'

'Oh, sure,' Andy agreed with a knowing glance at the children.

Alissa knew it was not for the children that the order was given and she gave Kieran a grateful glance. He just shook his head at her and helped her calmly into the helicopter. She assumed he was setting her a good example. It didn't help at all. She would have liked to cling to his hand, shut her eyes tightly and whimper. She was glad Kieran was sitting beside her and not taking a seat by the pilot. She really needed him.

Andy only had one spare set of headphones and when he looked round questioningly, Kieran pointed to James who soon had them fixed on his head and assumed an air of importance that had Kieran grinning to himself.

'Did you want them?' Kieran leaned towards Alissa and spoke quietly.

'No way! He already told me more than I wanted to know when he came to dinner.'

'I have advised him to be reticent,' Kieran said.

'Good! Let's hope he knows what that means,' Alissa muttered.

The engine started and that was the end of conversation because it was very noisy. It was a small comfort to know that if she screamed, nobody would notice much.

In fact, she would have enjoyed the trip had it not been for the knowledge that their destination was El Bueno. They skimmed out over the sea and came at the volcano from the other side and Alissa relaxed a little because it was an exciting and beautiful ride over the water.

The sea was peaceful, small waves dancing towards the shore flecked with white that rolled over the deep turquoise. At their own jetty, the sleek boat rocked at anchor, Harry and Greg were there and waved upwards to the children. In such a short time this place had become home, like her own private castle.

Alissa could see the house from this odd angle, the sandy beach where she played with the children and the graceful palms that grew to the water's edge. She could see her own room, the silky curtains blowing in the breeze, and when she glanced across at the volcano it looked beautiful, its sides clothed in forest with green fields on the lower slopes. Tranquillity cloaked the whole scene.

As they turned, she could see the village and then the helicopter began to climb higher and Alissa steeled herself for what she expected would be an ordeal.

The sands here were black, volcanic. A river she hadn't known about came into view. It snaked along, shining in the sun. Trees marched through the hills in the background and then...the volcano!

Sub-tropical vegetation covered the lower slopes, tall grasses waved by the river. The sun was behind the mountain, its fiery light outlining the massive shape. Beautiful, but from this side of the island, strange and almost alien. Once again she thought it was like a hidden land that time had passed by and forgotten.

Alissa bit down on her lip as the ground fell away, and almost before she knew it, the greenery disappeared and they were flying over harsh rocks and boulders that looked like a lunar landscape. She almost expected to see dinosaurs rearing up and trying to catch the tiny helicopter in their jaws. She was facing something that had seemed her enemy, from the first moment she had seen it.

The helicopter flew up the side and without warning they seemed to almost skim the edge of the crater. She knew without being told that they could have walked up here in comparative safety. She also knew that Kieran had given strict orders that they were not to fly over the crater itself and that if Andy forgot he would be sharply reprimanded.

All the same, she felt a terrible burst of fear and although the children were looking down in awe-stricken excitement, Alissa clenched her hands into two tight fists and stared down because she dare not look away.

Kieran reached across and took one of her hands. He gently but firmly straightened out her fingers and kept them warmly clasped in his own. With his hand engulfing hers, Alissa gave a breathless, shaky sigh as she tried to relax, but she didn't attempt to remove her hand from the warmth and comfort of his firm clasp.

'You can see it's quiet down there,' Andy yelled across the noise of the engine as he glanced back at her. 'The hot lava is quite normal and there's not too much of it at the moment.'

Alissa made herself look. There was not much lava, it was true. The red centre pulsed like a giant breathing but in the daylight it looked almost tame, nothing like the sort of inferno she had imagined. Small white wisps of smoke looked more pretty than intimidating. Slowly beginning to relax, she began to believe that she would escape with her life and live to laugh about the experience.

Suddenly the helicopter seemed to jump higher with no warning and hurled itself almost directly over the hot centre. Alissa leapt at Kieran and hung on tight. She didn't give a damn what he thought. She was safe with him and had no intention of letting go.

Immediately, Andy brought them back on course and they were once again skimming the edge.

'Thermal,' he shouted. 'Just a sudden up-draught.'

Alissa lifted her face that she had buried against Kieran's chest, seeking safety where she had instinctively expected it to be.

'I'm sorry.' She glanced at him in embarrassment, hoping he could read her lips. He just smiled at her and squeezed her hand and she took a deep steadying breath. She had survived and they were now skimming away, down the volcano on the homeward side, past more trees, more fields and then the sea and, best of all, the house.

'Home,' she said breathlessly and when she looked up, Kieran was watching her closely. He lifted his hand and ran it gently down her cheek. Not quite sure what he meant by the gesture, she was still too frightened to question it further, simply smiling back at him and deeply thankful when the helicopter began to descend. Her hand was still clasped in his and she didn't try to move it. She was grateful for his support and kindness. Without it, she would have probably screamed at least twice.

They all climbed out and the children instantly surrounded Andy and, much to his great delight, they were soon bombarding him with questions, especially James.

Kieran helped Alissa out, steadying her when her legs threatened to give way beneath her. 'You faced your nightmare. Was it worth it?'

'I don't know. Let's not do it again, though.' She was suddenly begging with enough urgency to have him looking at her worriedly.

'Maybe I should have made you stay behind,' he murmured.

She shook her head vigorously and met his intense gaze. 'I would have worried all the time you were away. It was better for me to be there.'

'Then we will most certainly not do it again.'

'Wasn't that great, Alissa!' James came up and to her great surprise and joy, took hold of her free hand. 'It's not so scary when you take a good look, is it?'

'Er…maybe not,' she agreed uneasily.

James looked up at her seriously and held her hand tightly. 'You won't have to fight it, Alissa,' he told her a little anxiously.

She knew what he meant and it warmed her heart instantly. He was actually afraid she would leave. She had succeeded in reaching James and he wanted her to be there.

'No, I expect not. It didn't look much on close inspection, did it? It was just like a fire that's going out, all glowing ashes and not too warm.'

He smiled up at her and then ran off to the house with Sally, both of them intent on telling Martha about the exciting adventure. Kieran had invited Andy up to the house for lunch and Alissa used the excuse to hurry off to her room to change. As she left, she could feel Kieran's eyes on her and she knew they were both thoughtful and warm. He too had noted the attitude that James had towards her. Her fright had been worthwhile after all.

Andy left after lunch and when they had all been to see the helicopter lift off, the children ran inside to change for the pool. Alissa went too, escaping with them before Kieran could speak to her. After this morning's episodes she felt nervous and shy. She was unable to forget how Kieran's arm had come swiftly round her when she had buried her face against him in fright. She had felt so safe and, much as she told herself that he was anything but safe, she still felt the warmth of his embrace.

When she finally got to the pool, the others were already there. Kieran, in black swimming trunks, was helping James to adjust his new equipment and Alissa went quickly to sit by Sally and admire her pretty new outfit.

'Does it look good, Lissa?' Sally looked up hopefully and Alissa helped her to fix the brim of the wide hat and assured her that it was all too beautiful.

Sally peered up at her. 'Why haven't you put your new bikini on that Daddy brought you?'

'He didn't bring me one. I told you he was joking.'

'He brought you that lovely bracelet instead,' Sally surmised.

'Yes, he did. It was very kind of him but I wouldn't wear it at the pool. I don't wear anything fancy when I'm swimming.'

In fact, she was wearing a black one-piece suit that looked very professional and Sally studied it thoughtfully. 'I'd better not take my new bikini into the water,' she mused.

'You could wear your other one and then put this on later to sit about,' Alissa suggested and Sally's face lit up when the way out of her predicament presented itself.

'I'll get it soon,' she promised, settling back regally.

'Another problem solved,' Kieran murmured, coming to sit beside Alissa. His glittering eyes ran over her slender figure in the black swimsuit. 'You look very professional.'

'Is this the part where we start to fight again?' Alissa looked at him over the top of her sunglasses.

'Not unless you want to.' He grinned at her and looked away. 'I suppose I was taunting again? With you, it's difficult to stop. Teasing you seems to have become a necessity. It takes my mind off the really urgent desire I have to kiss you.'

Alissa was in an instant turmoil because she also suddenly felt an urgent desire to be caressed by Kieran. She didn't know what to do or what to say. She just stared at him and he reached for her hand.

'Tell me you want me to hold you, Alissa.'

'I...I can't.'

All she could do was move and she jumped up instantly, greatly relieved to see that James was wading towards the deep end of the pool, making slow progress, walking in his flippers and not swimming at all.

She dived in, hoping she looked a proficient swimmer and not like a panic-stricken whale. The water cooled her and somewhat restored her equilibrium. When she surfaced, she saw James standing on the edge of the pool, looking down at her worriedly. Having donned his finery, he was too scared to stay in the water.

'Just fall in as usual,' she ordered, backing away and watching him with a confident expression on her face.

'Will I be all right, Alissa?'

She smiled up at him. 'No problem, you swim wonderfully. Pull your mask down and plunge in. Nothing to worry about. I'm here anyway.'

He nodded and followed instructions and, as he fell into the water, Alissa dived and followed him down, staying where he could see her. He panicked when water filled his mask but she brought him up and they stayed on the surface while she gave him a few added instructions.

He was soon skimming along with his breathing tube above the water and his eyes looking down at the bottom. Luckily, James was occupying all her time and gave her an excuse not to look at Kieran.

It was only as they both climbed out that Alissa became aware of a new arrival. Lara Fox was sitting by the pool, in a glamorous sundress, her eyes on Kieran and her face wreathed in smiles.

'Oh, crumbs!' James exclaimed crossly and Alissa had to admit that her own spirits had fallen to zero at the sight of the woman who was taking all Kieran's attention. 'Make her go, Alissa,' James pleaded in a whisper.

'Shh! We have to be polite to guests.'

'I wish we didn't have to,' he muttered. 'Now she'll stay on and on. You're the only one who can get rid of her. Do you have to be polite too?'

'Oh, definitely,' Alissa said, not feeling at all polite at that minute. Kieran looked only too pleased to have Lara Fox with him. He didn't look at all like the man who had wanted to kiss her only a few minutes ago, and Alissa had to work really hard on her smile of welcome.

Lara pushed her sunglasses to the top of her head and stared at Alissa, making notes it seemed of her figure in the black swimsuit, her long hair darkened by the water and her total lack of makeup. Apparently she was pleased to dismiss Alissa after a few searching glances.

'Why James,' she said patronisingly, 'You're learning how to dive, I hear.'

'I know how to dive,' James retorted stiffly. 'Alissa taught me. Alissa is an expert and she's my bodyguard,' he added, a threat in his voice.

'Really? Does she wrestle too?' Lara waved him away with a tinkling, dismissive laugh.

'She does karate,' James snapped, making it up on the spur of the moment. 'Don't you, Alissa?'

'Black belt,' Alissa agreed brightly, keeping her fingers crossed.

'How very frightening,' Lara breathed with a feminine shudder. 'I do hope you'll protect me, Kieran?'

'She's rarely violent,' Kieran assured Lara with a quick glance at Alissa. His lips were twitching with amusement and Alissa felt that she could have easily murdered him. He was enjoying this, she told herself grimly. But if he thought he was going to enjoy the sight of two women bickering over him, then he was very much mistaken.

'Let's go back into the water.' James clutched her hand and Alissa was only too ready to agree.

'And me,' Sally begged, edging away from their visitor.

'Change your suit then and join us,' Alissa told her.

'Oh, sweetie. That suit is so nice,' Lara crooned. 'Why bother to change into something less beautiful.' Her eyes skimmed over Alissa again and Sally rose to the occasion with no hesitation.

'Lissa and I only swim in real suits,' the child announced with a lofty air. 'This is for pretty. We wear black to swim. Real swimmers like Lissa do that.'

She marched off and Alissa dare not look at James. She

assumed he was giving his small sister full marks for a scornful attitude. She wondered how Kieran felt. If this little clash with the children had not shown him what they thought of his lady-friend, then nothing would.

'Let's dive properly in case she's watching,' James muttered. 'I want to show her that she's not important.'

'Can you do it, do you think?'

'If I hold my breath and really try,' he promised. Well that was what she had done this morning in the helicopter, Alissa thought and she nodded her agreement.

'OK,' she said. 'You first.'

He did very well and Alissa noted that Kieran was watching, his mind clearly not on Lara's chatter. He was much too interested in his son's progress. She couldn't help feeling elated as she dived cleanly in after James.

'We told a lie,' she whispered when they were once again on the surface and a good way out of the hearing of the others.

'I know. It was my fault,' James confessed. 'You were just sticking up for me. Can you do karate?'

'I'm afraid not. I don't think she can either, so we're fairly safe. But try not to drop me into the soup again like that.'

'I won't. I'll keep out of her way in future.'

Alissa bit her lip anxiously as she went to collect Sally who was ready for the water. Sally was now in a suit that was obviously too tight but it was black. She had evidently rummaged around in her things to make a point and Alissa gave her a quick hug as she held her in the water.

Of course, they had to come out sometime and, annoyingly, Lara Fox showed no inclination at all to leave. Martha brought out refreshments and Alissa sat as far away from their guest as she could, talking brightly to the children and trying not to hear anything that the adults were saying.

It would have been difficult in any case because Lara was whispering to Kieran, probably seductive sweet nothings, she told herself gloomily. The children were looking stony-faced. Their afternoon with their father was spoiled completely.

Later, Martha came out again to tell Kieran there was a phone call for him and he got up immediately to go into the house. It left Alissa to do the entertaining but it was very obvious that Lara did not intend to be entertained. She pulled her sunglasses back over her eyes and gave all the appearance of going to sleep.

'We can have one last quick swim and then I think we should be getting showered and changed,' Alissa told the children. They were both more than willing. Their enjoyment had stopped as soon as Lara Fox had arrived and they both walked with Alissa to the pool, James with a particularly grim expression on his face.

Lara didn't really know the children but Alissa did. If Kieran married this woman, James would make her life hell. Surely Kieran knew that? She would try to have them sent away, sent to some soul-less boarding school and Alissa's hands tightened at the thought. It would be the end of James.

As Alissa walked past Lara's chair, the unwelcome visitor made a great show of crossing her slender legs. One leg caught Alissa, tripping her. Alissa was quite unable to either side step or save herself in any way because it was so unexpected. She fell backwards and banged her head on the tiles at the edge of the pool. She blacked out immediately.

She came round to a terrible commotion. Sally was screaming hysterically and James was shouting at the top of his voice. Alissa lay still, too dazed to move, but James rushed at Lara who had sprung to her feet after her nasty little trick.

Alissa was vaguely aware of Kieran tearing round the corner but she was more aware that James had thrown himself at Lara Fox and seemed to be trying to push her into the pool.

'James!' She heard Kieran's voice crack out but James ignored it.

'She tripped Alissa,' he shouted, struggling with Lara Fox, showing no sign at all that he would let go. 'Alissa is hurt.'

Sally was screaming wildly as she tried to lift Alissa up, and Kieran clearly had his hands full. Martha ran out and order was restored as she took the children inside, leaving Kieran free.

He knelt beside Alissa and asked urgently, 'Where do you hurt?'

'I'm not sure.' She could only whisper and his hands quickly skimmed over her as he watched her face for any sign of pain.

'I'll have to risk lifting you. If anything hurts as I pick you up, shout out immediately.'

'Kieran,' Lara came forward and spoke to him but he didn't even look at her.

'I think you'd better go.' He spoke in a glacial voice. 'I'll speak to you later. Right now I have enough problems.'

'But I can help…' she began.

Kieran turned frosty eyes on her. 'I would imagine you've done more than enough already. Just leave us to cope.'

Lara Fox said nothing else and Alissa was too dazed to watch her as she left. The only glimpse she had of her was quite surprising. The glamour was a bit shattered. James had apparently been intent on robbing her of her sundress in his attempts to throw her into the water. As far as Alissa could see, the dress matched the sunglasses that were twisted and ruined.

Lara's high heels clicked angrily nearby, then faded away as she left but the children had evidently escaped from Martha because they both came racing back.

'Is she all right?' James hovered and asked frantically again, 'Is she all right?'

'She banged her head,' Kieran stated in his most matter-of-fact voice. 'Go to Martha and leave everything to me now.'

'Mrs Fox tried to hurt Alissa.'

'You told me and I believe you,' Kieran answered. 'Now let me see what Alissa needs to make her better. Go to Martha, both of you.'

'Will Alissa die?' Sally whimpered as she looked on with tears in her eyes.

'She wouldn't dare,' Kieran assured her, glancing down into Alissa's pale face. 'I absolutely forbid it. She's just dazed. Tomorrow she'll be fine.'

'If Mrs Fox comes again, I'll get her,' James muttered mutinously through his teeth. 'She was all sneaky but I'll be ready for her next time.'

'James,' Kieran warned. 'Go to Martha. If you want Alissa back then let me look after her.'

It was a stroke of genius and they both ran off quickly as Kieran turned his attention on Alissa. 'Now tell me what hurts. Does your back hurt?'

'No, not much. The thing that hurts most is my head. I remember banging it on the tiles.'

'Can you move your toes?'

'Sure I can – but why would I want to? I can move just about everything only don't ask me to nod my head.'

'Well, it seems that you haven't damaged your insubordination!' He lifted her gently and carried her into the house and up to her room. Her head was resting against his shoulder and although the pain was very bad, she felt too dazed to make a sound. She was safe again, almost comfortable with Kieran holding her. She hadn't expected to end up in his arms in precisely this way.

'Maybe it was an accident,' she managed to whisper.

'James said it was deliberate, therefore it was,' Kieran said.

'I didn't even see her move.'

'Then stop making excuses for someone you don't even like,' Kieran said in a driven voice. 'Concentrate on getting better. The children will be heartbroken if you have to go into hospital.'

'I won't!' She clutched his arm urgently.

'For once, you will do exactly as you're told.' He put her carefully on the bed and pulled a sheet over her. 'Until I can get the doctor here you'll have to stay in that wet swimsuit. We'll get you changed and take you down to the clinic when he's seen you.'

'Is there a clinic on Antarra?' A wave of dizziness affected her voice. 'Is it any good?'

'It had better be. I paid for it! If it isn't, I'll certainly want to know why.'

She hoped they had. For one thing, the thought of Kieran calling them to order was more than she could cope with at the moment. For another thing, she didn't want to be taken to a hospital miles away on the mainland.

She voiced this miserable thought. 'I don't want to go away, Kieran,' she said in a shaky voice and he came back from the door to sit by her.

'I'm glad about that.' His glance scanned her pale face, 'I definitely wouldn't be happy to let you go away.'

Alissa closed her eyes to escape the pain and immediately his hand touched her cheek gently. 'No sleeping,' he warned.

'The doctor has to see you first. Let me go and phone the clinic but just struggle to stay awake until then. We have to find out how bad that head is.'

'It's just a bump,' Alissa murmured, struggling to remain awake.

'Didn't I tell you to do exactly as you're told? No sleep, Alissa. Open your eyes and look round the room. I'll be back in two minutes.'

He went out and Alissa tried to obey. She assumed it could be dangerous to sleep after a blow to the head but it was so painful and sleep was so appealing. She struggled as much as she could but even so her eyes closed and she found herself drifting into the darkness whether she wanted to or not.

Kieran came back in and as soon as he saw her he sat beside her and lifted her up into his arms. 'Oh no you don't,' he said sharply. 'The doctor is on his way and you'll stay awake until he's seen you.'

'I can't!' She dropped her head on his shoulder and tried to sleep again.

'Yes, you can. Tell me about Lara. That should annoy you enough to keep you awake.'

'I think she tripped me on purpose,' Alissa murmured in a vague voice.

'I'm sure she did,' Kieran agreed. 'I didn't see it but I can imagine it very well. In any case, James said she did, therefore she certainly tripped you. He wouldn't lie.'

'We both lied today.'

'About the karate? I know.' He smiled down at her. 'I think we can forgive that though. James was trying to put an adult in her place with very few weapons to hand and you had to cover for him. We'll let that pass shall we?'

'The children are worried about her,' Alissa managed unevenly.

'There's nothing to worry about.' His hand gently stroked back her hair. 'We won't be seeing Lara again.'

'But what about after I've gone?' Alissa began to look agitated.

'Shh. We'll all go together, just like we did this morning. Now stop worrying. I can hear the doctor arriving. A few more minutes and then we'll have you changed and down to the clinic for an X-ray.'

'I don't want you to…' she began in an uneasy whisper.

He let her lie back on the pillows and looked down at her with glittering eyes. 'You don't want me to help you?' The softness in his voice made her tremble. 'Now why do you think I'm hanging round here so eagerly? You're a spoilsport, Alissa Brent.'

Even with a bad head he could still make her cheeks feel hot but she didn't get the chance to protest further because the doctor walked in with Martha, and Kieran had to step back and keep quiet.

The doctor thought Alissa would be fine but, even so, Kieran insisted on an X-ray, and Alissa found herself being driven to what turned out to be an astonishingly modern clinic in the nearby village. She didn't see much of it because by then she felt so bad that all she could think of was pain.

There was no fracture though, and when Kieran drove her back to the house he was fully armed with painkillers, both for the night and the next day. Martha got Alissa ready for bed and by the time Kieran and the children came up to see her, she was almost asleep.

Alissa heard Sally whisper. 'Will she be better tomorrow?'

'Not for a few days,' Kieran answered. 'Everyone will have to be very quiet until Alissa is better.'

James asked, 'Will Mrs Fox be coming back?'

He got a very determined 'No!' from his father. Alissa

couldn't tell whether James was disappointed or not. He seemed to have a lot of ill-will stored up against Lara Fox and Alissa could only hope that if the woman came back at all, Kieran would be on hand to deal with what she was sure would be further pandemonium.

At the moment though she felt too ill to try and hear more. She was aware that the children left the room quietly and she assumed Kieran had gone too.

It was rather nice to be cared about like this. She hadn't envisaged when she had taken this job that she would become so attached to her charges. She almost felt as if they were her own family.

Very soon though the job would end and then she wouldn't see them again. It hurt to even consider that. She wouldn't see Kieran again either with his astonishing eyes and his overwhelming ways. He came from a different world.

A few tears forced their way between her closed eyelids and hung on her pale cheeks. She was too filled with pain to lift her hand and wipe them away. It was terrible to think that when this was over, she wouldn't see any of them again, that she wouldn't be able look up and see Kieran. She might read about him in the papers or see him on television but he would not be real then. She just didn't want to leave him.

The tears trickled slowly down her cheeks and she felt a gentle hand on her face as Kieran wiped them away. He didn't say anything at all but she knew he was there. The tablets she had taken at the hospital were working more fully and Alissa let herself sink into the soothing darkness of deep sleep. This time, Kieran didn't try to stop her.

In the night, the pain woke her and she moaned softly, trying to turn. She was startled to see a figure detach itself from the shadows of the room. More startled still to find it was Kieran.

'What is it?' she whispered.

'Time for more tablets, I think.' He switched on a lamp and glanced at his watch. 'Just about time anyway.'

He reached for a glass that was beside her bed and counted out some white tablets from a box. Alissa lay watching him and he came towards her and carefully lifted her up.

'Just take these and then you can sleep again.'

Alissa obeyed unthinkingly. 'What time is it?'

'About two in the morning.' He seemed to be avoiding her eyes and she felt a burst of guilt that he should be here, taking care of her.

'I'm sorry,' she whispered.

'About what? You didn't fall deliberately.' He was still holding her and Alissa let her head fall against his arm. It was so comforting to be close to him.

'But you shouldn't have to be here, taking care of me. You're so busy and...'

'You prefer to have Martha?'

She tried to shake her head and gave a small whimper of pain that she couldn't quite disguise. 'No. She's busy too.'

'I see.' He eased her carefully down to the pillows and then sat on the edge of the bed and looked down into her eyes. 'You feel you should be abandoned? James wouldn't permit that. I almost had to fight him for the right to be here.'

Alissa didn't feel like jokes. She murmured fretfully and closed her eyes but she opened them again in shock when his hand gently stroked back her hair and he leaned forward to kiss her.

'Go to sleep, Alissa. Nobody would leave you to take care of yourself. Anyway,' he added, 'you're my responsibility and far too important to be neglected.'

She just looked up at him, her dark eyes searching his face and finding it so wonderfully familiar. He seemed to be searching her face too and he stayed there just watching her until her eyes slowly closed and she escaped back into sleep.

It was a couple of days before Alissa was anything close to normal, but after that night Kieran didn't sit up with her again. It wasn't necessary and she knew it but all the same, when she woke in the night she felt a small burst of disappointment that he was not there. She felt safe and comfortable when he was close and many times, Alissa lay awake wondering how it had happened that the man she had disliked so intensely had suddenly come to mean so much to her.

The children were allowed to come in to see her but Martha was always there to supervise and to make sure that they didn't stay too long.

'We love you, Lissa,' Sally said in her usual forthright way. 'You're going to stay with us for ever and ever now.'

'I only came for a little while,' Alissa pointed out gently, her hand ruffling the golden curls. 'I have another job that I have to go back to.'

'You can leave it,' James informed her in a firm, grown-up voice. 'We spoke to Dad about it and he promised to get it all sorted out very soon.'

Alissa was too startled to reply and, before they could say anything else, Martha came back to usher them out and bring a tray with Alissa's lunch. She was too bemused to eat very much and later when Martha collected the tray she gave Alissa a very anxious look.

'You've hardly touched this.'

'I know. I'm sorry, Martha.'

'Well, if you feel hungry later I'll bring you a snack.' She left, muttering worriedly.

chapter nine

A few minutes later, Kieran walked in looking almost as worried, his eyes going straight to her as she sat up in bed. She had a nervous expression on her face that made matters even worse.

'Martha tells me you hardly ate any lunch today.'

'I…I wasn't very hungry,' Alissa managed evasively.

'Do you feel worse?' He sat on the bed and looked at her with grave concern and Alissa felt extremely oppressed at that moment. She felt hemmed in and insecure about the future.

'No, I'm quite sure I'm ready to get up.'

'The doctor will decide that when he comes later,' Kieran announced implacably. 'Until then, you stay exactly where you are.'

Alissa looked away and nibbled at her lip and Kieran watched her closely.

'What is it, Alissa?' he demanded with his usual air of total command.

'The children said…I can't stay you know and they seem to be determined that I'm going to be…'

'A substitute mother? They care about you. Don't you care about them?'

'You know perfectly well I do!' Alissa glanced at him in annoyance.

He looked at her arrogantly. 'So, what's the problem?'

'The problem is that I'm here for a maximum stay of six months and then I return to my own job, my real job.'

'This is real. The way they love you is real.'

'Children are like that.'

'Not my children, especially James. Nobody has ever managed to get close to him before. He adores you.'

'He'll take to someone else sooner or later,' Alissa said, almost pleading with him.

'I very much doubt it. You've walked into his life and now you intend to walk out of it. It will be a blow all over again.'

'You're not fair,' Alissa protested tearfully.

He raised dark brows and pinned her with clear grey eyes. 'Why should I be? Nothing is fair as far as I can see. Why should I be the only one to have that virtue?'

'I haven't been unfair to you. Now you're making it impossible. You're making sure that when I leave I'll feel guilty.'

'Good!' He looked thoroughly satisfied. 'You have everything you want. You can have anything else you want. You're totally in charge and you're earning twice your normal teaching salary. At your age, that's fairly good going as far as I can see.'

'Then you can't see very well!' Alissa flared in frustration. "I have a life of my own. I am not a private tutor. I'm only here at all because you refused to take no for an answer.'

'All right,' he said, in what he seemed to think was a reasonable voice. 'Let's be sensible about this. You don't want to continue as a private tutor, you care for the children very deeply, the children love you and you've gone a long way already towards healing James. If you don't want to be a tutor, then stay as a substitute mother.'

Alissa felt as if she had been skilfully wound up into a tight knot. It was making her head ache again and he looked about as immovable as a mountain.

'What are you talking about?' She leaned forward to glare at him wildly.

'Marry me,' he suggested in the same reasonable but implacable voice.

Alissa stared at him, looking for some sudden burst of his weird humour. She couldn't see any sign of it. 'Are you mad?' she whispered, almost unable to speak.

'Definitely not. I'm exceedingly clever, according to most people. I spend my life making very astute deals. I'm making one now. Marry me.'

'Never,' Alissa choked, 'in a month of Sundays.' Her heart was beating so frantically she was sure it would be damaged. She should be as angry as she sounded but being strictly truthful with herself, she was not sure where the real anger was, or even if it existed.

He simply shrugged in a very unconcerned way. 'Think about it. You'll get used to the idea.'

'The idea, as you put it, is quite outrageous!' Alissa said this as forcefully as she could manage. She felt as if her bones were melting. She was scared, that was true, but she also admitted to a burst of excitement when he had made his startling offer. 'Just forget it. You can't just rope me in to your life.'

'Why not?' His amusement was very obvious. 'My ideas are always brilliant. I'm well known for them. This is one of my best ideas yet. It's foolproof. We all win.'

Alissa threw herself back on the pillows and forced herself to keep on glaring. 'Just in case you're serious and have not actually had an sudden attack of insanity, I flatly refuse the offer. Please go!'

'Of course,' he said with silky enjoyment, 'this is your room, after all. I wouldn't wish to outstay my welcome at the moment, not when we're in the middle of making an important deal.'

'There is no deal,' Alissa stated, almost shouting now.

'Forget all about it.'

'Most certainly not,' he stated, walking to the door. 'Not long ago you informed me that I refused to take no for an answer when I first met you. Obviously I'll refuse to take no for an answer this time. I want you to stay with me. The children want you to stay – and if you weren't so stubborn, you'd admit that you're happy with all of us.'

He left and Alissa realised she was shaking. It was impossible, ridiculous, and disgraceful. She closed her eyes but opened them almost at once. She didn't know if this was a dream or a nightmare. The thing that frightened her most was the certain knowledge that it was tempting. And that made her as mad as he was!

There was no doubt that she loved the children and was dreading having to leave them. There was no doubt too that most of the time now she watched for Kieran with excitement. She cared deeply for him. But to simply marry him in this cold-blooded manner? Why was she even considering it?

Alissa groaned and hid her head under the sheet. She was really worried about what he would do. Kieran did not accept defeat at all. He was powerful, a conqueror. He was Fate with clear, grey eyes. She refused to think any further. All this must be due to the sharp blow to her head. When she was really better, it would all go away.

When she was well enough to get up and resume her duties, Alissa found that Kieran was back to normal. He was busy almost all the time and every time she passed his study, the telephone seemed to be ringing. She began to think he had been intent on taunting her and nothing else.

In the evenings, too, when they ate together, he said nothing at all about his astonishing proposal. It went on like that for days until Alissa began to suspect she might have imagined it. She looked at herself worriedly in the mirror. Had she been affected by her fall at the pool? But if so, it was the only fantasy she'd had, since she had no problem in recalling everything else very clearly. In fact, as far as she could see, her brain seemed to be totally unaffected by the incident.

The children were delighted to have her back and she resumed the swimming lessons for Sally and the diving with James. She was quite touched when James asked her if she was well enough to continue. In fact, the children chaperoned her so carefully at the pool, apparently afraid that she would fall and bang her head again, that she found it highly amusing.

Martha beamed on her daily and it seemed to Alissa that her accident had brought about a great change in the entire household, as if some catalyst had been reached. Even Martha's husband George, whom she rarely saw, now made it his business to give her a cheerful smile each day. It was like being elected to some high office.

The only trouble was that she didn't know exactly *what* office, because she was quite certain that Kieran had not acquainted the entire household with his extraordinary desire to marry her. In fact, as far as she could see, he had completely forgotten about it.

Three days later, he brought the subject up again at dinner. Alissa had been too uneasy to simply walk out each evening and refuse coffee in the drawing room. Now he used the occasion to trap her.

'Have you thought any more about my suggestion?'

'What suggestion?' Alissa kept her voice steady, hoping he didn't know that her heart was pounding madly.

'I want to marry you, Alissa. What do you want to do?'

'I want you to stop talking about it,' she managed in an anxious whisper. 'You know perfectly well that it's a ridiculous idea.'

'I know nothing of the sort.' He sounded really surprised. 'You love my children, they love you. You would make a perfect mother for them. I can't think of a better idea.'

Alissa glowered at him. 'You're so cold-blooded! People don't get married for those sorts of reasons. Besides, I'm not an old maid, anxious to jump at the chance of looking after your children.'

He looked at her mockingly. 'What sort of reasons would you prefer for this marriage? I admit that you would have a ready-made family, but there's a lot of affection between you and the children. As to being an old maid...' He put his head on one side and inspected her sensuously. 'No, I don't think so. I can't imagine you ever being that, Alissa.'

'Please don't talk like this,' Alissa exclaimed, jumping up in agitation and getting ready to rush out of the room. 'You know I won't even consider the proposition.'

'It's not a proposition. It's a proposal. And just like any other man, I'm proposing to the woman I want to marry.'

'Stop it,' Alissa ordered desperately. 'You don't want to marry me. I can't take this seriously. Nobody would act like this. It's like something from the past, suggesting a marriage for the sake of two children. You'll meet someone else who will have all the attributes you need.'

'You have all the attributes now, Alissa,' he assured her softly. 'You've had all the attributes since the children took to you so firmly. I'm not just doing it for them, in case that troubles your conscience. I do intend to have a life of my own.'

'How?' She sank back to her chair and looked shaky.

'With you, of course. I want you. I've wanted you from the day I first met you.'

The blood seemed to drain from Alissa's face, her cheeks almost paper white as she struggled to comprehend what he was saying. It couldn't be true! Did he really mean...? 'You...you never said...'

'Of course I didn't.' He gave a wide, genuine smile. 'When I'm chasing after something, I don't show my hand, and you were obviously going to be hard to catch. I had to wait. Now I don't have to wait any longer. We can be married here – and the sooner the better!'

Alissa ran out of the room and he just let her go. She couldn't stop trembling because now she didn't doubt his determination to marry her. Her mind began to spin wildly from one thing to another, not daring to linger too long on any particular aspect of their relationship.

He had been very gentle when she was ill but, then again, surely anyone would have been? He had been kind to her when they had flown in the helicopter; had been *there* for her when she had needed him. He'd been annoyed when Andy Dodds had frightened her with tales of volcanoes, but taken all together, it didn't add up to anything other than a strong man protecting a woman. And any decent man would have done the same.

They wouldn't have kissed her though, would they? They wouldn't have watched her all the time, as Kieran seemed to do. But surely someone with so much desire would have spoken about it sooner? Have demonstrated his feelings in some way? The trouble was that Kieran was not like other people. His mind worked in an entirely different way. She didn't know what to do to get herself out of this predicament. She wasn't even sure if she *wanted* to do anything.

She could demand to go home, of course, but the idea of

leaving was not one she could bear to contemplate. She didn't want to leave the children and she had to admit that, deep down, she *never* wanted to leave Kieran. It was too frightening though. Where would she fit into his busy, powerful life?

Alissa was shocked that she had been considering his proposal so carefully. This was something she hadn't even thought of at all, and now she was turning the possibilities over in her mind as if they were very real.

Much later, almost one in the morning, she was no nearer to sleep than she had been when she had raced out of his sight and up to her room. She went down to make a drink, not a little annoyed when she realised that while she had been pacing about anxiously, Kieran had in all probability been sleeping soundly, his mind at rest after his astonishing declaration.

She took great precautions and didn't even consider making a cheese sandwich. There would be no entertainment for Kieran to walk in on tonight. A quick brewing of tea and then a rapid retreat. It was even difficult to keep her mind on what she had come down for, and Alissa knew she would be utterly jaded tomorrow. Kieran would be awake early and working from the word go, as well programmed as always.

She stood staring miserably at the kettle, willing it to come to the boil when a hand reached out and switched it off as two arms came round her from behind, without any sort of warning.

'Is it thirst, a headache or a nervous reaction?' Kieran asked quietly when she jumped and gasped at his unexpected arrival.

Alissa wanted to be angry and demand to be released immediately, but somehow the words would not come out. She seemed to be having difficulty breathing and when she just went on staring at him over her shoulder with a helpless look on her face, he lowered his dark head and caught her lips in a kiss so piercingly sweet and tender that she made no attempt at all to move away.

Helplessly submissive and trapped by her emotions, he had no problem turning her around in his arms, carefully drawing her closer to him. His hand cupped her head beneath the silken fall of her hair and he deepened the kiss slowly and insistently, his arms tightening around her until she was pressed close to his hard masculine body.

'It's all right, Alissa,' he murmured against her lips when she made a small anxious sound. 'I wouldn't let anything hurt you.'

'You could hurt me,' she whispered.

'Could I?' He drew his head back and looked into her eyes. 'For that to be possible you would have to care about me. Do you care about me, Alissa? Have you any affection left over from the amount you give to my children?' He let his eyes roam over her face and then come back to capture hers. 'Is there anything for me on the edge of the warmth you have for Sally and James?'

She meant to say no and pull away, but the feelings she had sensed since she had first known him flooded through her again, and this time she wasn't at all sure they were only sympathy. The hands that had been pressing fretfully against his shirt now curled into the material and she found it impossible to either draw back or look away from the grey eyes.

'You do care about me, don't you?' He didn't wait for an answer. The hard mouth relaxed into sensuous determination and his lips closed over hers again before she could even think of escaping. But she didn't want to escape. The heat that melted through her was inexplicable, flooding her whole being, reaching her toes and without even considering her actions, Alissa allowed her hands to creep upwards and circle his neck.

She could almost feel the triumph in him and his hand slid down her back, teasing every nerve ending until she was moulded to him, her softness blending with the taut muscles of his body. His lips began to trail over her neck, her ears, her eyelids and Alissa knew that the tiny little moans of pleasure were her own because she had never felt like this before in her life.

When his hand slid warmly inside her robe and searched beneath the lace of her nightie, she gave a startled cry that seemed to simply drive him on. His fingers closed possessively on her breast, teasing and soothing until she was gasping her pleasure against his lips.

'You like this, Alissa? You like me to touch you? I want to touch you. I want to feel you beneath me.' His voice lowered to a thrilling whisper against her mouth. 'I want to be inside you, to possess your beautiful body, to feel you clinging to me in the night.'

She was crying without tears, cries of excitement that sounded loud and desperate to her own ears and he swept her up into his arms, his lips teasing hers as he walked from the room and climbed the stairs. When he took her into her own room and placed her on the bed, her arms still clung tightly to him and he slowly released them, holding her hands in his and looking down at her.

Softly against her ear he said, 'You would let me take you now, wouldn't you? You would come to my bed and stay there, let me love you all night. I want to, Alissa. I want to just as much as you do. Marry me and you can have anything you want, anything I can give you. We can all be happy. I'll treat you like a queen.'

'I…I don't want to be treated like a queen.' Tears streamed down her face in reaction to the sexual storm that he had produced inside her.

'But that's how you will be treated, I'll never tire of making love to you.'

'You don't love me,' she sobbed. 'This isn't love.'

'It's the nearest thing that most people achieve.'

'You thought you loved your wife,' she reminded him desperately.

'Cynthia very soon shattered my illusions on that score. Once Sally was born, she made it very clear that I was no longer of any interest to her – other than providing her with a wealthy life-style, of course,' he added wryly. 'She desired money and she saw me as her meal ticket. I dearly love my children – but I paid for them the hard way.'

The even, unemotional words stopped Alissa's tears like a flood of icy water.

'And now you need somebody to look after them?' she said quietly.

'I need *you* – and I want you for *myself*,' he ground out with sudden harshness, sitting down beside her and gathering her up into his arms. 'The fact that the children adore you is merely a bonus. I want you with me every day and in the night – every night, Alissa!'

'And what about what I want?' Alissa was desperately frightened when she felt her body beginning to melt towards him once again. 'I want more than a terrifying automaton.'

'Terrifying?' He suddenly relaxed, grinning into her face. 'If I kissed you again you would let me pick you up and make love to you, right now. I'm going to marry you, Alissa. One way or another it's going to happen,' he added softly. 'Because I want you – and I want you so badly, that I'm not prepared to let anything stand in my way. So don't let that fact slip from your mind. I wanted you from the moment I saw you with your sister. I didn't know then exactly who you were, but I had every intention of finding out. London and your sister are now a long way off.'

'Are…are you threatening to…to simply seduce me?'

'Yes.'

When she stared up at him in horrified astonishment, he laid her back down on the bed and rose to his feet with one lithe movement, his face struggling with laughter.

'Go to sleep my beautiful battle-axe,' he ordered with a grin. 'In the morning, we'll set the date for our marriage.'

'No,' Alissa said sharply, trembling all over again.

'Yes,' he corrected, flashing her a glance that seemed to set her on fire. 'Surely you must know by now that I always get my own way? So "yes" is the only word I'm prepared to accept. You can even forget the rest of the English language. All you'll need to do is to admit that you want me too. And know that I'll take care of you, because you will then be mine.'

He just walked out, smiling at her from the door as if she had already agreed and then leaving her in peace. But she knew she would not have any kind of peace. One thing was for sure – she wasn't going to sleep at all.

She was quite right. She hardly managed to close her eyes all night. And in the morning, Kieran took one look at her pale face when she came down for breakfast and then left her alone. He kept out of her way all day and Alissa assumed he was letting her come to terms with what he had apparently decided was to be her fate.

She was quite capable of talking herself into a sensible frame of mind until she saw him, and then the memory of the night before simply overwhelmed her. It was no use pretending. She knew exactly how she'd felt last night, filled with a thrilling, overpowering emotion for the first time in her life. She had never before faced such internal turmoil.

She had been too busy being brisk and businesslike, too determined to make something of her life. All she knew about men she had read in books. A modern virgin! Alissa grimaced. In some obscure way, Kieran had saved her from herself, because she might very well have been feeling a lot more than pale and tired this morning.

During the day, the children were strangely subdued and Alissa could not come up with any good reason for this. There was an air of unease everywhere. Perhaps, if it had not been for the children, she would not have paid much attention because she was feeling distinctly uneasy herself. This could not account for the children, however. When she asked them what was wrong they just didn't know.

At dinnertime she faced Kieran with it. 'The children have been behaving strangely today,' she said when he sat without speaking. 'Have you said anything to them?'

'About us? Of course not. I'll tell them when there's something to tell. We'll both tell them.'

'There won't be anything to tell,' Alissa warned, her face flushing under his sudden stare. 'And this can have nothing to do with our…our problem. They're both a little strange.'

'We don't have a problem,' Kieran said firmly. 'We know exactly what we're going to do. All I'm waiting for is the date and time of the ceremony – and that's entirely up to you.'

'I can't go on holding this sort of conversation with you. You've decided what you want without even considering my feelings. Sexual desire is simply *not* a good enough basis for a marriage,' Alissa said agitatedly, jumping to her feet.

'Well, we're at least making some progress,' Kieran

taunted as she made her way to the door and safety. 'Normally you just storm out.'

'I'm afraid to do that now,' Alissa snapped. 'Especially when it appears that you're deranged!'

He merely smiled at her with so much possessiveness that she was glad to escape. In fact, she didn't really want to go to her room, she thought miserably as she stared out of the window. She wanted to sit and talk to him quietly, to get to know him better, but quite obviously that was proving to be impossible. He had stated his case quite clearly. She was good with his children – and he wanted her. That was all.

The heat that came instantly to her face died very rapidly when she saw a sudden burst of activity from El Bueno. There was a great puff of white against the dark sky, the smoke rising higher than it had ever done before. The pulsating red that was reflected in the velvet blackness of the night was more pronounced too. And for the first time there was a low rumble of sound, so slight that she would have missed it had her ears not been so constantly attuned to the danger of the mountain.

Alissa moved to the balcony and watched, waiting for the sound to come again and when it did she was so afraid that she went to find Kieran, with no other thought in her head but his comforting presence.

She saw the light under his bedroom door as she walked on the darkened passage and she knocked with no hesitation whatever. She needed him and he was there. He was always there.

When he opened the door she took no notice of his surprise, and when he saw the expression on her face, he asked quickly, 'What's wrong?'

'It's the volcano. Something's happening. I don't know

what, but I know that I'm scared and probably likely to be mistaken. All the same, I don't like the way it's behaving.'

He stared at her for a second and then drew her into his room, closing the door and walking with her out on to his own balcony. The curtains were closed and he opened them as he switched off the main lights.

'It looks all right,' he pointed out. 'Just the same as usual.'

'Wait,' Alissa begged, 'you'll see in a minute.'

They waited, Kieran with a good deal of patience as he obviously expected nothing to happen. When there was the same large outburst of white smoke, and the same increase in the pulsating glow, he was instantly alert. When it happened again a few minutes later, Kieran walked to the phone without a word and dialled a number.

'What are you doing?' Alissa asked anxiously.

'I'm going to set your mind at rest, one way or the other. You've been afraid of that damned thing for far too long. Either we convince you that it's safe or we leave here.'

'We can't,' Alissa said quickly. 'We're still hiding.'

'No, we're not,' he corrected, his eyes softening at her total commitment to the children's welfare. 'I told you that we'd tracked down my ex-wife's brother. By tomorrow we should have more news. I'm now almost certain who's behind this, so we can leave whenever we like.'

He turned back to the phone when it was answered and it was obviously Andy Dodds because Kieran started in right away with sharp questions, listening intently and then questioning again. When he put the phone down he turned to Alissa with a determined look.

'According to Dodds there's definitely increased activity. He says it's probably safe but we're not about to take his word for it. Dodds is so enamoured of that volcano he would probably be content to watch it erupt and take snapshots while the island burned.' He walked towards her and stood with his hands firmly on her shoulders. 'Tomorrow we're pulling out of here.'

'Are you sure? Don't let my worries influence you.'

'I wouldn't make much of a husband if your worries didn't influence me,' he said quietly.

'You…you're not my husband,' Alissa pointed out shakily and he smiled down at her with a sensuous look on his face.

'I am going to be, Alissa. We both know that. I've found you and I want you too much to ever let you leave me.'

When she continued staring up at him, he pulled her to him and enclosed her firmly in his arms. 'Now,' he said softly. 'Let's plan. Tomorrow we leave and then we'll all be safe from the volcano. In the meantime, if anything happens, don't forget that we have the boat all ready and waiting. I can have us all out of here and well out to sea, in just a few minutes.'

'Suppose it happens sneakily?' Alissa worried, biting anxiously at her lip and making no attempt at all to extricate herself from his arms. He didn't laugh at her. He simply reached out one hand and lifted a two-way radio microphone beside his bed.

'Greg,' he said into it. 'Are you there at the boat?'

'On deck at this minute. What's happening?'

'At the moment, nothing. Get Harry and take it in turns to watch the volcano all night. There's extra activity. In the morning, we'll be pulling out. Take turns to keep an eye on it until then, one of you staying awake at all times.'

'Will do.' There was silence and Kieran replaced the hand-held radiophone in the case beside his bed.

'He didn't ask any panicky questions,' Alissa muttered as Kieran's arms once more tightened about her.

'He'll panic with the next man if the volcano blows. Until

then, he'll watch with Harry. In any case, if there had been immediate danger, Dodds would be ringing everyone on the island. You can sleep in peace.'

Alissa nodded doubtfully, still biting at her lip and he tightened his arms.

'Sleep with me, Alissa.' His hand lifted to cup her face gently.

She looked up at him and was instantly lost. She had never had an affair in her life. Hadn't even thought of it, because there hadn't been anyone who'd even remotely excited her. Now, however, she wanted to stay with Kieran, and not because she was scared of the volcano.

The tension in the air that had been disturbing the children had got to her too. But the feelings inside her were nothing to do with that and she knew it. The seductive words he had spoken to her before came swimming back into her mind, overwhelming her and she swayed towards him.

He caught her closer. 'Stay, Alissa.' He whispered the words against her trembling lips. 'Let me keep you here and love you all night. I want you, I need you close to me. I want you in my bed, in my arms. I want to sleep with you, wake up with you. I want to feel you against me.'

She couldn't answer but she moved further into his arms, her lips lifting for his kiss and he swept her off her feet as his mouth opened over hers in a deep, drugging kiss that melted her even more.

By the bed, he let her feet touch the ground and steadied her when she swayed. She was light-headed, utterly lost and he knew it perfectly well.

'Not because you're afraid of the volcano,' he warned thickly. 'Not because you just don't want to be alone. If it's that, I can sit downstairs with you and talk all night. This has to be because you want me.'

With a small whimper of sound deep in her throat, she let her tongue slip over her suddenly dry lips and his eyes fastened on the innocently sensuous movement. He bent his head and let his own tongue follow the same path, slowly and seductively. 'Because you want me, Alissa,' he breathed into her mouth.

She tightened her arms round his neck, giving in to the burning rush of desire. 'Yes,' she whispered. 'I want you. I want to stay with you.'

'Then you're going to marry me soon,' he promised as his hands began to move over her possessively, 'because once I've taken you, I won't let you go. I need you, Alissa. I need you so much. Tomorrow you'll be mine permanently.'

Permanently. It was thrilling and frightening all at the same time. She wouldn't have to leave Kieran again. She would always be able to look up and see him. Alissa dared not think further than that, dared not imagine what it would be like to stay in his powerful world for the rest of her life.

There was now, however, and it was all she could think of. She moaned softly as he undressed her and let his lips trail seductively over every part of her skin he uncovered. His hands cupped her breasts as she clung to him and his tongue brought the rose pink centres to sweet stinging life.

'Kieran!' She gasped his name and he held her tightly, looking down into her wide, dark eyes.

'I am not going to hurt you, darling,' he promised. 'You're safe with me, my beautiful Alissa. I know you've not done this before. Trust me.'

She did trust him. She knew she had always trusted him, even coming here in the first place had been an act of faith and now she was placing her whole life in his strong, capable hands.

He lifted her on to the bed and looked down at her as she

lay there. Then he pulled his shirt over his head and began to undress. She closed her eyes tightly, too shaken to watch further and as he came to her and took her back into his arms she turned to him anxiously.

'Shh,' he whispered against her lips. 'Everything will be as slow or as fast as you want it to be. I've waited for you for weeks. I can wait longer.'

The words drew her back into the heated excitement. Had he waited for weeks? Had he wanted her for so long a time? When he kissed her before, had he wanted to end up here in his room, in his bed?

Alissa murmured in a rush of incredible delight and reached up to kiss his cheek but he didn't want such chaste kisses. He took her face into his hands, his mouth devouring her as his body moved slowly against her own.

The sensuous, demanding movements enraptured her and she clung to him tightly. When his hand moved to caress her and his fingers gently probed the heated centre of her being, she gasped against his lips and his tongue slid hotly into her mouth, slowly exploring the dark warmth as his fingers explored the moist heat of her most secret place.

Burning ripples seemed to spring from every part of her and she moved against him, begging for more of the magic and he slowly moved her closer but she could not get close enough. She murmured against his lips, fretful and anxious, her hands beginning to explore the taut muscles of his back, the strong power of his legs.

The power thrilled her, his hands thrilled her even more and she tore her lips away to cry out demandingly, 'Kieran. Please!'

'Not yet,' he breathed. 'Wait, sweetheart. I'm not going to let you be hurt. The first time is going to be magic.'

It was magic already to Alissa. She was totally without

control, her body demanding more from Kieran, her breath a wild gasp in her throat. When he moved over her, she parted her legs to get him closer, moulding herself to him with an action that showed her own desperation and he lifted her closer still until they seemed to be simply one person.

She threw her head back and his lips trailed kisses over her slender neck, his hands running over her body with renewed urgency. 'Now, Alissa,' he demanded, 'I need you now.'

When he pushed inside her slowly and powerfully, she tensed up but the pain was a momentary flicker, her sharp cry as much rapture as anything else and his lips covered hers in a burning kiss as his body claimed her own.

'Forever,' he breathed into her mouth. 'Forever, Alissa. Promise me.'

'I promise,' she agreed frantically. 'Please don't stop, Kieran.'

'Nothing in this world could stop me now. You belong to me.'

'I want to.'

'I know, sweetheart.'

He began to move inside her, building up the excitement and the pleasure until she felt herself spinning into brilliant lights, her wild cries lost against his lips. There was so much joy, she felt she would die right there and all her worries were forgotten as she left the world in his arms, moving into a timeless place but knowing he was there with her.

She loved him. If she had ever doubted it she knew for sure now. It was only partly the pleasure, the excitement. It was Kieran. Love flowed through her, making her soft and willing, her body enclosing him with warmth and she heard his groan of satisfaction as his taut muscles relaxed against her.

She held him tightly as the world stopped its dark, frantic spinning, and when he raised his head to look down at her, she ran her hand gently across his forehead, her eyes on the shining strands of black hair that had fallen over his face. She couldn't smile. The feelings were too deep.

'Alissa?' He voiced his concern at her silence.

'Please don't ever move,' she whispered. 'Just let's stay here like this until we die.'

The taut expression left his face like magic and his own hand came up to stroke back her fair hair, his eyes roaming over her flushed face. 'It's better to start again each time,' he said thickly. 'I haven't thought that before but, with you, it's better to enjoy everything again, right from the beginning.' He held her gaze with darkened grey eyes. 'Nobody has ever given me so much before. I wanted to take you but you simply gave me everything.'

'I couldn't help it.' She smiled then, shyly and he moved from her, clasping her in his arms when she cried out in protest.

'Why do you constantly say you're fierce?' he laughed softly. 'You're warm, Alissa. You're warm to all of us and, now, warmer than ever with me.'

'There's nobody here to fight,' she murmured dreamily. 'I feel safe.'

'You are safe,' he assured her, tightening her against him. His lips nuzzling her neck, his teeth nipping at her skin when she sighed with pleasure. 'You're safe until I want you again.'

'That's safe,' she murmured. 'It was safe and…and wonderful. I wanted to stay there always.'

'Oh, Alissa!' He moved over her quickly, kissing her with growing urgency. 'You don't even know how to protect yourself from me.'

'I don't want to. Is that bad?'

'No, Alissa,' he whispered. 'It's good. You bring happiness all the time and now you're mine, aren't you?'

'Yes.'

'Don't ever leave me, Alissa.'

She looked up at him and saw the lingering traces of anxiety. He was so masculine, so strong and beautiful, but now he looked like James. He looked as if he could be hurt.

She put her hands at each side of his face and looked deeply into his eyes.

'I won't leave you, Kieran. This is not something that I could do if the thought of leaving you was inside me. I trust you completely. Trust me too.'

He said nothing. He only looked into her eyes and drew her tightly to him, holding her and planting kisses on her face and neck.

'I want to feel you against me in the night,' he finally said huskily. 'I want to listen while you breathe. I want to know that you're there, near me – mine. I've never wanted anyone as I want you. Make me gentle, Alissa. Give me back my life.'

She melted against him, willing to be swept back into the wonder and passion that overwhelmed her, but this time his kisses were soft and warm. His lovemaking brought tears to her eyes and, all the time, Kieran looked down at her tenderly, no longer the harsh and powerful man she had met such a short time ago.

He kissed the tears away and gathered her close.

'Now we'll sleep,' he whispered. 'I wanted to watch you while you slept, but this time I'll probably sleep with you. I'm content, Alissa. Tell me you are too.'

She smiled into his eyes and stroked her hands down his face.

'I'm content,' she murmured. 'We can both go to sleep.'

'Be there in the morning,' he whispered.

'Where would I go? I'm exactly where I want to be already.'

chapter ten

The ringing of the telephone awoke Alissa early the next morning and when she opened her eyes, Kieran was almost dressed. He was just pulling a soft, blue sports shirt over his head as he came to answer the phone. He sat on the edge of the bed and reached for her, pulling her up into his arms as he picked up the receiver.

She leaned against him, relaxed and happy as she closed her eyes and remembered how he had reached for her in the night, whispering her name, stroking her body and wanting her again. She could feel the same need pulsing through him now as he kissed her ears and her eyes, a sound in his throat like the purring of a satisfied tiger.

Kieran trailed his lips over her face but he suddenly stiffened and spoke sharply. 'Immediately. Ignore us. We don't need you.'

He put the phone down and turned Alissa's face to his. 'Get dressed. And don't go looking for particular clothes. Just pull on anything.'

'It's the volcano.' Her heart gave a frightened leap and Kieran nodded.

'That was Dodds. They've gone straight up to Alert Level Four from more or less nothing happening. He says that's a remarkable sign of instability. Apparently, Level Four gives us forty-eight hours but Dodds is worried. He's flying now, getting the island cleared, getting people to their boats and warning everyone. More experts are on their way but we're not waiting.'

While he was speaking, he gathered Alissa's clothes from

where they had been dropped the night before. He tossed them on the bed and she pulled them on with no embarrassment whatsoever. In the first place, things were too dangerous for foolish coyness and, in the second place, they had been wrapped close together all night, talking and making love.

'The children!' She looked up in alarm but Kieran was already at the door.

'I'll get them started and then you can take over. Grab anything that's precious to you but don't waste time packing. We may not have any time at all.' He opened the door and then muttered to himself and came back to the radiotelephone. 'Greg, are we fuelled up?'

'Maximum capacity.'

'Then start the engines and stand by. Send Harry up here with the poke. I want to be leaving in fifteen minutes or less. The volcano is probably going to blow.'

'*Christ*!' Greg just switched off and Alissa knew he would already be taking action. Kieran's men did not hang about discussing orders. She knew their transport to the boat would be here almost at once. She ran her fingers through her hair and as Kieran left the room she was right behind him.

She dived into her room and dressed rapidly. The children were already awake but still in bed and Alissa rushed in to get them ready. 'Rise and shine,' she ordered brightly. 'No time to wash. In ten minutes we're off the island.'

'Where are we going?' Sally rubbed the sleep from her eyes and Alissa had to make a quick decision. She decided as usual that the truth was unbeatable.

'The volcano is acting a bit strangely,' she said as she lifted Sally up and began to dress her quickly. 'We may be going home, but at the very least we're going to pull out to sea.' She glanced across at James who was watching her with intent dark eyes. 'Can you see to yourself, James? We're in a bit of a rush this morning.'

He nodded and sprang out of bed, dressing in front of her with none of his usual stiff embarrassment.

'We only take what we would hate to lose,' Alissa pointed out.

'My new bikini and hat,' Sally decided at once.

James was ready with remarkable speed and he already had his new diving equipment under his arm.

When Alissa looked up, Kieran was in the doorway, his eyes on her. He seemed to have heard and he nodded with approval. 'Are we ready?'

Alissa smiled across at him and put Sally into his arms as she took James' hand in hers. 'All set. Let's party,' she ordered gaily. James grinned up at her and Kieran smiled into her eyes.

'That's my girl,' he murmured and for Alissa it even wiped out the fear of the volcano.

On the way to the stairs, she darted back into her room. Kieran called to her at once, a definite note of anxiety in his voice but she was out in a second, the box holding her bracelet in her hand.

'I'm not leaving this. If I can't change my clothes until we get to London, at least I'll look good in my bracelet. Sally can wear her bikini and James can wear his mask and flippers.'

They raced down the stairs. Martha and George were waiting on the step.

'All your lovely clothes left behind,' Martha commiserated as they went to the waiting poke.

'She can spend a whole week shopping when we get back to London,' Kieran muttered, struggling to get them all into the vehicle at once. 'Let's go.'

Alissa looked at her watch, somewhat surprised she had remembered to put it on. 'Just under fifteen minutes,' she said briskly. 'We must do this again sometime and try to improve our record.'

'Shut up, Alissa,' Kieran ordered but he was laughing all the same and James crushed up to her, grinning widely, still clinging to her hand.

They were all safe for now and Alissa stole an anxious but secret look at El Bueno. It didn't look any different at all but she was glad to be leaving it behind and, as far as she was concerned, Andy Dodds was the expert. If he had said 'go' then he had meant it. He loved the fiery mountain. He would not have ordered evacuation for nothing.

She wondered if he would stay behind to watch? The helicopter had seemed to her to be a very flimsy craft. But the people she loved were with her now, safe as far as she could tell and soon they would leave Antarra behind, at least for a little while.

Greg Snow was waiting by the boat with the engine started and Kieran had everyone on board speedily. He didn't even glance at either the volcano or the house.

As Greg backed the boat away and turned for the open sea, Alissa asked Kieran, 'What about your things?'

'I closed down and finished any transmissions this morning before you were even awake. All that's left is a quantity of electronic equipment. It's set up in every place I go.'

Alissa wasn't really listening. She was looking at him with a sort of numb disappointment. 'You did all that while I was asleep?' she whispered. 'You knew about the volcano?'

Kieran turned to look down at her, his face darkening when he saw her reproachful eyes.

'You heard me get the message. You were right there with

me, if you recall. I closed down because I had every intention of getting you and the children off Antarra today. It really
wasn't worth all the worry it was causing you and there was
no reason to stay once Cynthia's brother had been found. I
did intend telling you, of course, and giving you time to pack.
I hadn't actually planned this urgent retreat.'

His grey eyes held hers, ignoring her flushed face and her
apologetic glance. 'You still don't really trust me, do you,
Alissa? You give yourself to me like an angel but when the
world stops spinning, you're ready to throw those rocks
again.'

'I'm not, really I'm not,' she promised miserably. 'I don't
know why I asked you that. I heard you get the message.
It…it's just that…I expect I can't believe it.'

'Believe it. When we get home, we'll be married in days.
Or have you changed your mind about that?'

'No,' she whispered and Kieran gave her a very decisive
smile.

'Very wise, because I certainly haven't changed my mind.
We'll tell the children as soon as they're settled.'

'All right,' Alissa agreed in a subdued voice.

'No caustic comments or fighting remarks?'

He was back to being sardonic and she felt a wave of anger
that quite wiped out her feeling of regret at her momentary
lack of faith. She said nothing but he obviously saw the
feeling flash in her dark eyes.

'Back to normal, I see. You only behave sweetly in bed
then? That's all right. We can cope with that.' He was looking
at her seductively now and Alissa wondered if he was just
doing it to punish her. At any rate, it changed her feeling of
hurt to anger.

She spun round and went to see to the children, leaving
Kieran to stand by Harry at the stern of the boat, a look about

them that told her they were still worried.

In spite of the fact that they were now well under way, Alissa had the same uneasy feeling. She fussed over the children for a while but as Martha and George were already doing that very well, she went back on deck, her eyes on the fast retreating island.

Kieran was watching through binoculars and when he spotted Alissa looking rather bereft he signalled her to come to him. As she came near, he reached for her, putting his arm round her and handing her the binoculars.

'Are we safe now?' She asked the question quietly but Kieran did not deal in soft words and speculation.

'I think so but really I don't know. I haven't paid a great deal of attention to volcanoes and what they do when they explode. Perhaps it will be nothing at all.'

He sounded doubtful and Alissa bit down on her lip and tried to remember how far away they had been when they landed by air at the other island. She hadn't really tried to locate exactly where they were. The days had simply flown along and now she felt as disorientated as she had been when they had first arrived on Antarra.

How far was far enough? None of them knew. Even Andy Dodds would not know because this had taken him by surprise. It might be a very violent explosion.

'Take a look.' Kieran glanced down at her as she stood without lifting the binoculars to her eyes. His voice had softened from his previous anger and she knew it was because he felt her fear.

When she looked through the lenses, Antarra seemed to leap out at her. El Bueno was very active. There were no longer the delicate wisps of white smoke. The sky over the island was dark, almost like night, the hills around black, and white steam was rising in a towering cloud from the volcano.

'It looks…angry,' Alissa whispered and, once again, Kieran's arm came round her shoulders as he pulled her close.

'We're moving away fast,' he assured her in a low voice. 'Perhaps we'll not even see it go, if it eventually does. According to Dodds, the activity can stop as suddenly as it starts.'

She knew he was merely trying to calm her fears. If he had been at all happy about the volcano he would have given them time to pack. Alissa stared through the binoculars, mesmerised by the beautiful mountain that had frightened her since her first sight of it. 'At least we're all together,' she whispered.

'Don't be frightened,' Kieran said softly, tightening his arm round her shoulders. 'It might not happen, Alissa.'

She hoped not but suddenly, the white cloud was rising like an exploding bomb and the violent blast followed almost immediately, echoing across the water and rocking the boat.

Alissa let the binoculars fall from her eyes, her hand holding them feeling quite limp. A flash of flame and then awe-inspiring, boiling, spectacular clouds filled the sky and spread out rapidly. The original towering cloud looked like the aftermath of an atomic explosion and without any aid from the binoculars, she could see fire and dark ash fountaining into the air above El Bueno.

More explosions followed and as the children rushed on deck with Martha and George, they all saw the first burst of fiery, glowing lava begin to pour down the mountainside. The scene was like some heavenly fireworks display, a firestorm of awesome power like the wrath of some angry god whose fury drove him to destroy everything.

Rivers of brightly glowing lava, more wide and fast flowing by the second, raced down the mountain towards the sea. The clouds boiled in violent frenzy and jagged bursts of lightning crackled round the summit of El Bueno.

Alissa swallowed her fear and looked again through the binoculars. It was raining ash and mud and the rivers of fire were advancing at a terrifying rate. The first tower of cloud was now miles wide on the top of its slender column and although the boat was speeding away, she still did not feel they would be far enough from the gases and the falling ash and rocks.

She could see the children were also mesmerised by fear. 'James? Come and look,' she suggested, steadying her voice. 'This is not something you'll see again at close quarters.'

He came forward warily and Sally too came to them, to be swept up into her father's arms and held safely.

'You were right to be scared of it, Alissa,' James said in a frightened little voice as he stared through the binoculars.

'Oh, I'm very clever,' Alissa told him cheerfully. 'We're safe now. It's a good distance away and it can't run after us. It's quite spectacular though, isn't it? We'll never forget this. I wish we had a camera but mine's back at the house.'

She began to explain to him all the things that were happening, searching her memory for Andy Dodds' words that night at dinner.

The house, so grand, so beautiful. It would be crushed and burned in the path of the lava. Nothing would be left of her newfound happiness. The volcano would ruin the island. Their tranquil beach would be gone.

Kieran took her hand. 'We're all together,' he said softly, reading her thoughts. 'There'll be another place, another time.'

Alissa tightened her hand in his. They were all together and nothing else mattered.

'Lara Fox,' she said, suddenly remembering.

'She left the island while you were ill. I spoke to her that night. She went back to England as far as I know. At any rate, she not on Antarra.'

James stood watching El Bueno, taking it all in, more excited now than frightened.

'Alissa, it's fantastic. I wonder if Andy is getting aerial shots? I can still see his helicopter flying over the sea.' He swept the binoculars around and stopped suddenly. 'I can see the other boats. They're going the wrong way.'

'They're going to the mainland,' Kieran told him.

'It's not smooth there like it is here,' James mused aloud and Kieran took the binoculars from his hand and focussed. He turned urgently to Harry.

'Huge waves,' he said quietly. 'Tell Greg.'

Harry took one look at him and went quickly to the other end of the boat. Kieran sent the children back to Martha and George.

'What is it?' Alissa asked when they were out of hearing distance.

'I'm not sure,' Kieran muttered. 'These waters are usually tranquil but there's a lot of turmoil close to Antarra now.'

'Tidal wave,' Alissa surmised in a whisper filled with dread.

'Probably not but we'll put on speed anyhow.' Even though the children could see them, he drew her close, his arm once again round her shoulders. 'You're a wonderful girl, Alissa. I know how frightened you are but still you calmed James and even taught him something. I wish to God I hadn't brought you out here.'

'Then I wouldn't have known you,' Alissa pointed out softly. 'In any case, you don't take no for an answer. It was all inevitable.'

'Have I ruined your life?'

She looked up into the silvery grey eyes for a second. 'No. Whatever happens, I'm glad and I'm happy. If it were not for that damned volcano,' she muttered. 'I never trusted it and *now* look what it's doing!'

Kieran suddenly laughed, his eyes roaming over her irritated face. 'We've got to tell the children soon. I want to kiss you soundly but I think they've had enough shocks for one day.'

'So has Martha,' Alissa murmured, noticing Martha's eyes thoughtfully regarding them as Kieran stood with his arm tightly round her shoulders. 'I think she's drawing her own conclusions.'

'Without doubt,' Kieran murmured. 'Martha knows me well enough. She knows I'm not normally given to displays of affection, except with the children. Let's go forward and urge Greg on.'

Alissa gave a last worried look at the island and another at the sea. So far the waters were calm but she would not feel safe until they were once again in the air and on the way home. She gave a great sigh.

'Now what?' Kieran asked quickly, turning toward her. 'Your sighs worry me. They invariably make me feel guilty.'

'I was only thinking that I'll have to go and stay with Candy and Bob after all.'

'Until the wedding? No way! The children would riot and so would I. You don't leave my side until you have my name and, even then, not often.'

It brought a smile to Alissa's gloomy face and he urged her forward with him, his hand on her arm. In spite of everything, the feeling of safety flooded back into her. Kieran had no intention of letting her go and she didn't want to go.

He may not be in love with her but he needed her. So did the children. She was where she wanted to be, at least she *would* be when they got out of this predicament.

From then on, there was just a feeling of a race against time. She didn't know anything at all about tidal waves following a volcanic eruption but she knew they existed. She had painted very frightening pictures in her head about the volcano and now it had happened. She began to paint other pictures. Her mind began to see giant waves that would come in a rush and swamp the boat and, although it was all probably foolish, Alissa was praying for the sight of the other, larger island as she listened to the engines racing flat out.

When their goal eventually came in sight, they all breathed a sigh of relief but Kieran was still tensed for action and action was what they got as soon as they landed. His plane was already on the tarmac, the car waiting at the harbour and Alissa knew he had made these preparations before she was even awake.

They were quickly rushed away and in so little time that she felt breathless, all Kieran's party were safely on the plane and the pilot ready to taxi to the end of the runway.

'Take off,' Kieran ordered sharply and Alissa could see why. There was a sudden flurry of activity around the buildings and, although she didn't know exactly why, she knew they must get clear immediately.

The plane turned and picked up speed, moving down the runway like a sprinter in a desperate race and leaping into the air. Alissa's tight shoulders relaxed. They were safe.

As they banked around the airport and climbed, she saw the first rush of waves approaching the island, not too high and probably not be too damaging, but as far as she could see, the runway would soon be too deep in water to allow any flights out.

Kieran's plane climbed rapidly and they all had their last glimpse of El Bueno. It was distant but burning against the darkened sky with a display of hot ash, and showers of burning rock tossed hundreds of feet into the air. A firestorm of breathtaking proportions. The lava glowed orange and red, fierce burning rivers that sprang from the heart of the volcano. The original cloud was now dark and had spread to the island below them, it's advance terrifyingly swift but they were safe, flying away from the fountains of fire.

Alissa clutched Kieran's hand as he sat beside her.

'We made it,' she breathed shakily. 'We're safe!'

James came scrambling across and managed to make room for himself between them. Sally sat on her father's knee.

'It was a close thing,' James said to Alissa. 'I'm glad I had time to collect my diving things.'

'It was scary,' Sally pointed out in a frightened little voice. Kieran hugged her close.

'It's over now,' he said softly. 'We're all going home.'

They watched Antarra until it was out of sight and Alissa wondered what Kieran's thoughts were at this moment.

After a while, James asked, 'Will the house have burned?' His thoughts like Alissa's were back on the island.

'Perhaps,' Kieran said quietly. 'It's a pity because it was beautiful but we'll get another house, on another island if you like.'

'I was happy there, this time,' James pondered. 'It would be nice to have somewhere warm to go to.'

'Not *that* warm,' Alissa murmured dryly. 'Next time we'll avoid volcanoes. We're facing nothing that isn't scared when I throw rocks at it.'

'Are you staying with us, Alissa?' James was instantly alert, a tremendous hope in his eyes but it was Kieran who answered.

'Forever and ever,' he said, looking at Alissa. 'When we get home, Alissa is going to marry me.' He lifted her hand to his lips to make sure the children were very certain of his meaning. 'We won't be managing without her again.'

Alissa looked at the children uneasily but she need not have worried. Their unexpected silence was not disapproval. They were watching her with glowing eyes.

'Great,' James shouted suddenly and he threw his arms round her neck as he kissed her cheek.

'I'm going to tell Martha,' Sally announced importantly, scrambling from Kieran's lap and moving back to where the others were sitting.

'Me too,' James stated. 'Greg and Harry will want to know.'

'And the whole universe,' Kieran observed dryly as the children rushed off to spread the news. He took Alissa's hand in his. 'Any regrets?'

She shook her head, too filled with happiness to speak.

'James kissed me,' she whispered when she felt able to put her feelings into words. 'I was worried he might not like the idea.'

'He loves you, Alissa,' Kieran said quietly and she wiped frantically at her eyes, determined not to be silly about this. Kieran hadn't added that *he* loved her and perhaps he never would, but he would always be with her and so would the children.

She managed to compose herself and not a moment too soon. The others made their way along the plane to offer congratulations and it was some minutes before they had everyone settled again with James and Sally sitting opposite, talking excitedly to each other.

'Well, *that* upstaged the volcano,' Kieran said. 'Pity we didn't have champagne ready. Never mind, we'll do that at home.'

And it was there again, that word 'home'. She hadn't had a real home since her teenage years. While they had been on Antarra, she had settled into the security of knowing that the house and the island were home but it had only ever been temporary.

Alissa glanced at Kieran secretly. Last night she had been in his arms and with the powerful dominance that was so typical of him, he had swept her permanently into his life. She still didn't know what she was to him. He wanted her, he needed her and she was suitable because the children loved her, but what else? As far as she knew, there was nothing else and that was a knowledge she would have to live with.

'You'll not be hurt,' Kieran's dark voice said as if he was reading her thoughts again. 'I promised you, Alissa. I keep my promises.'

Alissa said nothing because what was there to say? And after a second he took her hand and locked her fingers with his. 'Try to sleep,' he suggested. 'There's been a lot of drama today and last night you had very little sleep.'

That was more than enough to have her closing her eyes firmly, hoping he didn't notice her flushed cheeks and after a while she slept, her head sinking to his shoulder as he moved her more comfortably close.

Kieran did not sleep. He wasn't thinking about money or clever deals, he was thinking of another woman whose head had once rested on his shoulder. He was thinking of Cynthia. His glance moved to the children who were also sleeping and finally his own eyes closed as he completed his plans.

It had been a pity about the volcano, too soon but it didn't matter. He let his face rest against the silky head at his shoulder. *This* woman wouldn't ever betray him. She would stand by his side always. Angry or gentle she would always be there. He trusted her completely just as the children trusted her. He could reach for her in the night, see her face every morning. She had banished loneliness from his heart.

Alissa had only briefly been in Kieran's London home before. Now she was coming to live here permanently and even the children seemed to be looking at her anxiously.

'Come in here,' Kieran ordered when the children had been taken off by Martha to change from their warm climate clothes into something more suitable for the coolness of England. She had announced too that she was going to see them into the bath and then let them have a good long nap.

It left Alissa free and as she followed Kieran into his private den she felt jaded and most definitely the worse for wear. She had no clothes here and she was quite embarrassed about her appearance. At the airport it had not really mattered. Everything Kieran did was private and one of his cars had been waiting for them. There had been no reporters to question them about their escape from a volcanic explosion.

She faced Kieran now though and she hadn't missed the worried looks James had bestowed on her. She stood waiting for anything that Kieran might say with such a resigned look on her face that he sighed and shook his head in exasperation.

'Come here, Alissa.' He leaned against a huge desk that seemed to dominate the whole room and when she walked slowly forward he reached for her and pulled her against him. His glance moved slowly over her, summing up her strange mood.

'Do you feel trapped? I've forced you into this, pressurised you and now I feel as if I've captured an unwilling slave, a wild thing who is going to pine away in captivity.'

'I'm not,' Alissa protested, surprised at his astute assessment of her mood.

His hand tilted her downcast face and he searched her expression intently. 'Are you sure? I took you to Antarra knowing I had a daily fight on my hands. You were like a beautiful, untamed creature, ready to defend yourself from me and defend the children from anything. I look at you now and see a timid person, more girl than woman. Have I done that? I know what I'm like.'

There was regret in his voice as if he now wished things had not worked out as they had and Alissa met his glance with a fear of her own that had nothing to do with being captured. 'Don't you want me now, Kieran?'

He pulled her to him with a swift, fierce movement, parting his legs to move her even closer.

'Every minute. Every second. Even if you've decided you don't want to be with me, I still want you here.'

'I want to be here,' Alissa assured him with a wan little smile. 'I expect I'm tired and the children were looking at me as if I didn't belong, especially James.'

'He's scared you'll leave,' Kieran informed her in the same husky voice as before. 'So am I.'

'Do you want me here so much?' Alissa looked up at him as her face started to come to life.

He clasped her face in his hands, kissing her deeply and then pulling her head to his shoulder. 'You crazy, mixed-up girl. You beautiful madwoman,' he said roughly, his hands tightening on her. 'Of course I want you here but I don't want you crushed and lifeless.'

'I wouldn't permit it,' Alissa muttered, yawning against his chest. 'I feel weary though, washed out and slightly scruffy.'

Kieran laughed and lifted her away from him, the harsh

anxiety gone from his face. 'I'll show you where you'll sleep,' he said and when she looked up in surprise he added, 'until we're married.' He grinned at her woebegone expression and led her out of the room, his arm firmly round her.

'I haven't any clothes with me,' she reminded him when she had inspected the luxurious bedroom she was to have for her own. 'Most of my things are at Candy's. I didn't leave much at the cottage.'

'Give me her number and I'll ring her while you sleep,' Kieran offered. 'I'll get one of the men to drive over and collect your clothes.'

'She'll attack him,' Alissa muttered, yawning again and walking into the shower room to turn on the water. 'She's very protective of me. She didn't want me to go with you and when she finds out about the volcano, she'll spring into action.'

'I know. I'll have to chance it.'

'I've got nothing to sleep in either,' Alissa complained and Kieran turned to the door.

'One more word on that subject and I'm going to stay. Go to bed. I've got other things to do and they won't wait. You stay here until we're married next week but I'm making no promises that I'll stay in my own room.'

Alissa gave him a sleepy smile and he groaned but left the room all the same. She showered and almost fell into bed, her mind too tired to be anything but hazy about the future. Kieran would care for her as much as he was capable of doing and the children loved her. There would be happiness and most people didn't even achieve real happiness.

She drifted to sleep with the picture of the volcano swirling round in her mind, the boiling clouds of smoke, underlit with red, the rivers of fire and the surging fountains of burning rock and ash flung upwards with unimaginable force.

There were hidden fires in Kieran too, fires she hadn't once suspected when she had first met him. Life with Kieran would be bliss or misery and she still didn't know which of these was her fate. But she loved him and it was enough.

As Alissa had suspected, her sister created a fuss but Kieran dealt with it smoothly. He invited Candy and Bob to dinner that night and allowed the children to stay up as they had slept for most of the day.

He had not slept himself apparently because when Alissa awoke, her suitcases from Candy's were in her room. As she finished dressing, Kieran knocked on her door and came in to speak to her.

His gaze ran over her appreciatively in her wine-coloured dress that fitted smoothly to her hips and rounded breasts. Her hair was washed and shone in the lights and after staring at her in his usual unnerving way for a second, he came forward and pulled her almost roughly into his arms.

'You're so beautiful,' he murmured against her lips. 'I'm not sure I'll let you leave the house in case you run away.'

'I won't run away,' Alissa whispered and he stared into her wide, dark eyes, his momentary tension relaxing.

'Just in case you consider it, I want you to wear some identification.' Before she could question him, he took her hand and slid a huge diamond ring on her finger. Alissa looked up at him in a sort of wonder. 'You would soon be found if you were wearing that,' he assured her. 'I got it while you were asleep. It identifies you as mine.'

'I don't need any identification, Kieran. I won't run away and get lost. I don't want to be anywhere but here with you.' She took her courage firmly in hand. 'I love you.'

'Alissa,' he said thickly but there was no chance to say

more. There was a flurry of knocking on Alissa's door and the children ran in.

'We've got visitors,' James said in an anxious voice. 'There's a lady who says she's Alissa's sister. Is she coming to take Alissa away?'

'She is not,' Kieran informed him. 'Stop worrying that Alissa is going to leave us. She's here forever.'

James still looked anxious and Alissa went to kneel in front of him, her arms going round him. 'I won't ever leave, James,' she said firmly, gathering Sally close too. 'Next week you can come to the wedding. In the meantime, look at my ring.' She held her hand out to show them the glittering ring and Sally was filled with awe, her worries forgotten.

'It's my engagement ring,' Alissa told them. 'It means that I've promised not to leave any of you. I don't break my promises, you know that.'

When they left, Alissa turned to Kieran with a rueful smile. 'It will take a long time with James,' she said quietly.

'Not for you.' He held her close for a minute and then gave a sigh. 'Come on. There's no getting away from your sister. I have to go down and be inspected and I dread to think what her reaction will be when she discovers that you're going to marry me. You'd already convinced her that I'm to be avoided.'

'It was a long time ago,' Alissa said softly.

It seemed like a lifetime ago. Now she was committed to this powerful man who led her to the door and walked beside her. She felt the weight of the ring on her finger and it gave her the confidence she needed.

Alissa need not have worried. The children were already charming her sister and brother-in-law and Kieran set out to charm too, putting on an act that had Alissa smiling to herself. He had no intention of having her lured away, neither had the children it seemed.

The house and the housekeeper also impressed and after a rather grand dinner in sumptuous surroundings, Candy murmured her approval. There was not much doubt about Bob. He was getting along famously with Kieran and Candy followed Alissa up to her bedroom to freshen up when the children had at last gone to bed.

'What did I tell you?' Candy looked triumphant. 'I distinctly remember saying he was a gorgeous man.'

'And you were right,' Alissa admitted, hiding her smile.

"I don't like to think of the danger you were in when that volcano erupted though,' Candy muttered, determined to worry about something. 'If Kieran hadn't been there, I shudder to think what would have happened.'

'If Kieran hadn't been there then I wouldn't have been there either,' Alissa pointed out.

'I suppose not,' Candy mused. 'It's wonderful to think you have a ready-made family,' she added, brightening up. 'It's easy to see that Kieran dotes on you.'

Alissa smiled but said nothing. She supposed he did dote on her in a way. There was no doubt that he wanted her but she wondered how long that would last? He wouldn't ever leave her, she was sure of that, but how would she feel when he no longer looked at her as he did now? She kept her worries to herself.

When Candy and Bob left much later, Kieran gave a greatly exaggerated sigh of relief. 'I think I passed the test. At least she didn't question me vigorously, although she certainly stared at me for a long time when she arrived.'

Alissa grinned. This was all new for someone like Kieran who made his own rules. He had spent the whole evening wondering if Candy would strongly advise against him and apparently it had mattered.

'You're accepted into the family,' Alissa assured him. 'Candy will now take your side in any future arguments. That's how it works.'

'You and I will fight in private, as usual,' Kieran murmured. He reached for her and pulled her into his arms. 'The children are asleep. Martha is off-duty and I haven't held you close for ages.' He swung her up into his arms. 'Your place or mine?'

Alissa wrapped her arms around his neck and buried her face against his shoulder as he carried her from the room.

'The first place we come to, the nearest place,' she whispered.

chapter eleven

In Kieran's bedroom, he began to undress her. He didn't speak but his eyes held hers all the time, even though he wanted to look at every part of her he uncovered. He could feel tension in her and for all his strength and power he didn't yet understand this woman he had captured.

She could be fierce and gentle, angry and tender. She was breathtakingly beautiful and her loyalty humbled him. She had gone with him to Antarra and faced everything she had because she felt she was needed.

He wondered if she knew how much he needed her.

Alissa shivered as he drew her close. His hand curved under her hair as his fingers soothed at her nape and his lips closed over hers. It was so erotic standing pressed against his clothed figure while she was naked and when he ran his hands over her, searching and arousing, her arms wound around his neck as if she were in a dream.

By the time he lifted her on to the bed she was in a golden trance, her eyes unable to look away from him. Not a word had been spoken but words were not needed. He had aroused her with his fingertips, seduced her with his eyes and when he came to her she couldn't find the strength to lift her arms.

He wanted to hear the words she had spoken earlier. He wanted to hear her say she loved him, wanted it with a desperation that made him tremble but she said nothing and he made love to her until sleep claimed them both and was content to hear her quiet breathing in the night.

Somehow that night changed everything, as if some hidden lock had been turned in a secret door. Kieran's teasing stopped. The way he looked at her was different. The way he touched her as they passed was different. Alissa felt he needed something from her but she didn't know what it was and Kieran was not going to tell her.

Several days later, Alissa was sitting in the drawing room when James came in. She was still teaching the children until Kieran deemed it safe for them to return to their school, but this was a break.

She was looking through the morning papers as she drank her coffee and she smiled as James walked into the room. Like his father who asked without speaking, James sat facing her and said nothing.

Finally Alissa put the paper down when it became obvious that he wouldn't tell her his latest problem.

'Did you want to speak to me, James?'

'No.' He blushed and then changed his mind. 'Yes.'

'I'll listen,' she assured him gently, knowing that something important was troubling him.

'You'll think I'm silly.'

'I doubt that. You're not silly. I'm much more silly then you. Why don't we give it our best shot?'

He nodded in his usual grown-up way but his eyes were wary. 'I wanted to ask you something,' he said quickly. 'How much do you think I'm worth?'

Alissa was quite taken aback but she tried to keep the surprise out of her voice. 'Do you mean as your father's son or are you talking about the various treasures you have in your room and hidden in the boxes in the playroom?' She was very brisk about this, seeing it was important to him for some reason.

'No, I don't mean that,' he replied after some thought. 'If you were selling me, how much would you ask for me?

That's what I mean.'

Alissa managed to hide her amusement and looked serious as she considered. 'I see. You mean weight for weight, overall value, like selling a pig or something. Let's think.' She put her head on one side and looked him over carefully. 'A pound of sugar, I believe.' He stared at her as if she was mad. 'No, on second thoughts, that's too little. A pound of sugar, a pound of butter and a jar of strawberry jam.'

James just went on looking at her.

'Then again,' she said quietly. 'I wouldn't even consider selling you even at such a price. I can manage without sugar and butter and I absolutely hate strawberry jam. I couldn't manage without you though, James. If anyone asked to buy you, I'd shout at them even if they really wanted you. I'd get the biggest stick you've ever seen. I'd chase them up the street, beating them all the way. Greg and Harry wouldn't have time to help because I would be too angry to wait for help.'

Tears came into his eyes and he jumped up and rushed across to her, flinging himself at her and winding his arms round her neck. 'Oh, Alissa! You're the funniest person in the whole world.'

'Well, my mother was funny too then.' Alissa rocked him close, resting her head against his. 'She used to say I was worth a pound of butter, so you see, you're worth more than I am.'

'What was your sister worth?' James looked up at her with tears on his face.

'Cheese, but only half-a-pound.' She ignored the tears. He was laughing now and whatever had been troubling him was gone for the time being but the tears still streamed down. 'Don't mention it to Candy though. After the wedding, she'll be your auntie. You'll also have an Uncle Bob and some cousins.'

'What are the children like?' James wiped the tears with the back of his hand as he sat beside her.

'Quite nice little pests. You'll probably like them.'

She gave him a quick kiss as he went out again and it was only then that Alissa realised Kieran had heard the whole thing.

He was standing at the other door, the one that led into his own private den and he was looking at her with such an expression on his face that she stood quickly.

'What is it?'

'It's you.' He came towards her and hugged her close. He buried his face in her hair and held her tightly. 'You're not just the funniest person in the world, Alissa. You're the most wonderful, the most remarkable.'

'What did I do?' She drew back to look at him and his hand trailed gently down her face.

'You said the right thing as usual. James has a long memory. The night Cynthia left, she made a bargain with me. She offered to give the children up without a battle. She didn't care about them but she was their mother and she knew her rights. She offered to keep silent, to make no claims for custody or visiting. In return, I was to give her money. She even knew how much with no bargaining necessary.'

Alissa stared up at him with saddened eyes. She knew now why James had asked her that strange question, even without Kieran telling her.

'I asked her how much her children were worth,' Kieran continued bitterly. 'She said two million each. Then she thought longer and said James was probably worth more because he was older and a boy. She wanted three million to give up rights to James.'

'She sold them to you?' Alissa's question was a horrified whisper.

'Yes. That's how it came out. I accepted because I didn't want the children involved. I was terrified of losing them to her. We were standing in the hall and she was about to go for the last time. She walked out with my cheque in her hand and a smile on her face. When I looked up, James was at the top of the stairs listening. He was only five but he was very bright. He knew. He hasn't spoken of it since. Speaking to you was the first time he has ever come close to mentioning it.'

Tears were streaming down Alissa's face and he held her close, comforting her as she was comforting him.

'I wish you'd told me before,' she sobbed quietly.

'Oh, no, Alissa. You clearly didn't know when James asked you that question. He's not stupid. You answered straight from the heart and he knew at once. He knows you wouldn't ever give him up, and he knows you would fight for him with your big stick and your fierce temper. He knows you love him and so do I.'

He rocked her close, his face still against her hair and she wanted to cling to him with all the fierce protectiveness in her nature. Now she knew how much Kieran had suffered, how much James had suffered. She wouldn't ever let any of them go.

'Don't ever try to get rid of me, Kieran Tempest,' she said passionately, her eyes filled with tears. 'If you do, I'll take that big stick to you too.'

'I couldn't have enough of you, sweetheart.' His hold on her tightened almost to the point of pain. 'We all need you. Anyway,' he added with a wry look at her, 'I suspect that if you left the children would go with you.'

'And you. We'd tie you up and take you along. James would help me.'

'And Greg, Harry and Martha,' Kieran laughed. 'I expect I'm stuck with you?'

'True,' Alissa agreed with the sound of tears still in her voice. 'Don't you forget it.'

'I'll not forget it.' He smiled down at her. 'My fiery angel,' he murmured, his eyes searching her face. 'Whatever happens, I have you, we all do. You have enough fire to warm us all to the heart. I'll protect you all my life and I know you'll be right there beside me, stick in hand, shouting.'

'Believe it,' Alissa muttered, her lips still trembling.

'I do,' he said as his lips covered her own.

The wedding was quiet, almost a secret affair because neither of them wanted the interest that followed Kieran about. They chose a small church, well out of the City, and the only guests were the people closest to them, the members of Kieran's household staff, Candy and her family.

Bob gave Alissa away and Sally was proud as the smallest bridesmaid. James was proud too, standing at the church door and then seeing people to their seats. It was all secret and beautiful, and afterwards they had a wedding lunch at Kieran's house with Martha beaming at them and hovering round to make sure everything was all right.

It gave the children time to get to know their new relatives and after the day was over, both Sally and James expressed their satisfaction at the new turn of events.

'They're OK,' James told Alissa smugly as she tucked him up in bed.

'I'm glad you like them. They're a bit noisy, don't you think?'

'It's because they're small,' he reminded her in an indulgent manner as he turned over to go to sleep. 'I bet they can't even swim yet.'

'Probably not,' Alissa agreed, wanting James to retain his superiority. He was smiling as she left the room and when she got outside, Kieran was waiting for her, lifting her up into his arms and striding off down the long corridor to his room.

'Your things have been moved. You're with me.'

'So who's arguing?' Alissa reached up to kiss his face. 'If you're looking for a fight though…'

'I can think of much better things to do.' He slid her to her feet inside his room. 'This is our wedding night. I was afraid it wouldn't happen. I wanted to cover the bed with rose petals but you would have laughed.'

'I wouldn't,' Alissa whispered, looking up at him. 'It would have been old-fashioned and wonderful but Martha would have had to clear them all up in the morning. I'll just imagine them,' she said dreamily as he began to undress her.

Later, as they lay contentedly in each other's arms, she brought up the subject of the children and their education.

'Is it safe for them to go to school? I don't mind going on teaching them but they should be mixing with other children. You saw how they enjoyed being with Candy's little brood today.'

'I noticed.' Kieran's stroked her gently. 'They can't go yet though.' He tilted her face up. 'Cynthia is in London.'

'When?' She was instantly anxious and raised herself up to look down at him.

'Since yesterday. I didn't tell you before the wedding because I didn't want anything to spoil it. My people got news of her arrival as soon as she landed. As yet, we don't know what she's up to, but I can guess.'

'She's after the children.'

'And she's not going to get them. Stop worrying, sweetheart. She can't touch them because this time I wouldn't pay her off. I'd fight her out in the open. I have you now and the children know they're loved. She hasn't seen them for three years. She wouldn't stand a chance.'

'But if she tries to kidnap them.'

'Then I'll see her in prison. I'd even see her in hell for what she did to James. Sally wouldn't even recognise her. She's played right into our hands because she's being tracked now and when she leaves here, she'll be tracked to wherever she's living. From then on she'll be watched, for the rest of her life if necessary. You can forget her.'

Alissa sank back to the pillows and tried to relax again. She wished she could forget Cynthia. The woman was like a black cloud at the back of her mind. She lay stiff and anxious, thinking furiously, but Kieran turned her towards him, his hand covering her breast and his lips seeking hers.

'Keep teaching the children for now. When we've got Cynthia sorted out, they can go back to school. After all, I don't want a teacher. I want a wife and you'll be having children of your own.'

'I will,' Alissa promised, 'and we'll love them all. But Sally and James are our children already. They'll never be less to me than that.'

A few weeks later, Cynthia arrived with no warning. Kieran was out in the City and the children were having their lessons. It was mid-morning and as Alissa came down the stairs for her short break, Martha answered the front door. Cynthia was there, standing on the step, as beautiful as Alissa had already seen from her photographs and quite sure of herself.

'Mr Tempest is out,' Martha snapped, making no move to invite the woman inside.

'I only came to see my children. Step aside, Martha. I know my way around this house.'

'You can't come in when Mr Tempest is away,' Martha

averred, standing her ground. 'I'll not have you causing him any more grief, just when he's happy.'

Alissa had been standing quite still, almost eavesdropping as James had done so long ago but now she came down the stairs and into view. 'Let her in, Martha. If she wants something, I'll deal with her.'

'Yes, Mrs Tempest.' Martha moved aside. 'If you want me…'

'I do, Martha. Go up to the children and see that they stay exactly where they are, even if you have to lock them in. There is no way they're going to see this woman.'

Martha hurried upstairs, her face a picture of anger and satisfaction and Alissa came into the hall to face the woman who had wrought such havoc in Kieran's life and the lives of his children.

'You have two minutes to say your piece. After that you leave. But understand this clearly. You are not seeing the children.'

'You may be Kieran's wife now,' Cynthia snapped, 'but the children are mine.'

'No, they're not. You sold them. What's the problem? Did you spend the money? They're not for sale now. You can't sell something twice.'

'I want to see them!' Cynthia's face was red with anger and Alissa looked at her steadily.

'Over my dead body,' she stated through clenched teeth.

'We could arrange that.'

Cynthia took a step forward, leaving room for two men to enter the hall. They were big men, burly and rough looking. Alissa didn't know if one of them was the notorious Uncle Carl and she didn't care. It looked as if she would need that big stick but she didn't have one with her at the moment.

If she shouted, the children would hear and want to come.

James must not see this woman in his vulnerable state. Even if they attacked her, Alissa knew she would fight to the last breath. Now she only had her anger as a weapon.

'Get out! You're all trespassing.'

'I'm not,' Cynthia pointed out with a satisfied smile. 'You invited me in.'

'I thought that rule only applied to vampires. You're just a greedy human being.'

'I'm the children's mother and these are my friends.'

'I can believe it. They look just your style.'

'Find my children,' Cynthia ordered, turning angrily to the men.

They stepped forward but Alissa moved to block their way, bracing herself for a battle she could not hope to win.

'Stay right where you are.' Greg walked into the hall from the kitchen, Harry beside him. They looked exactly what they were – dangerous men – and Alissa breathed a sigh of relief.

Greg spoke into his portable phone. 'Mr Tempest,' he said laconically, 'you've sure got some unwelcome visitors here.'

The men with Cynthia looked as if they were thinking of making a break for it but Harry fixed them with thoughtful eyes.

'You could try it,' he suggested. 'You wouldn't get far and it's more comfortable in the house. We wouldn't want to break all these nice things would we?'

They just stood still and in a few minutes, Kieran's car drew up outside and he was coming up the steps. His eyes went to Alissa as soon as he was in the hall.

'All right?' He addressed Alissa with a trace of anxiety.

'Perfectly.' She wanted to fly into his arms and hit him all at the same time because he must have known about this. 'The children are with Martha and know nothing at all. It would perhaps be a good idea if we went out of the hall to a more private place.'

She led the way to the drawing room, her posture stiff and angry.

Kieran watched her for a second and then indicated the door to the others.

'Inside,' he ordered, with a contemptuous glance at his ex-wife. 'You came here without an invitation. You'll leave when I've acquainted you with my terms.'

Later, Alissa thought she had never heard such quietly spoken threats. Even though they were not directed at her, she felt her blood run cold and the men with Cynthia had no doubts about their fate if they ever tried to come near any of Kieran's loved ones again.

Greg and Harry escorted them to the door and Kieran turned to the woman who had once been his wife.

'From now on,' he promised savagely, 'you will be watched wherever you go. I have wealth enough and determination enough to have you followed for the rest of your life. The children don't know you and they never will. Alissa is my wife and she loves them. They love her too and they won't ever have to fear desertion and hurt. I'm letting you go but return to England again and I'll know it instantly. By coming here you've risked imprisonment and the only reason you're escaping is because of the children. Next time, there'll be no escape.'

'I only wanted to see them.'

'Liar,' Kieran said contemptuously. 'You want what you've always wanted, the only thing you've ever wanted – money. Your brother finally confessed. I have his written statement that you and a certain acquaintance of mine planned to kidnap the children. Come back to England again and I'll see you in prison. Kidnapping is a serious offence. I don't think you'd like prison very much, Cynthia. Now get out of my house and just pray that I never see you again.'

After Cynthia left, Alissa was silent, then she turned to Kieran as he stood angrily staring out of the window.

'You knew,' she accused quietly. 'You knew they were coming.'

'I didn't,' he said without turning round. 'I knew she was in England. I told you that. I also knew she was in London. I went to get her this morning but we couldn't find her.'

'We?' Alissa didn't suppress the anger in her voice.

'I've got other people besides Greg and Harry,' Kieran said, in what she took to be an off-hand manner.

'You could have told me where you were going,' she pointed out in the same angry voice.

'There was no need for you to know.' He sounded rather dismissive and Alissa's ready temper began to rise with some speed.

'Greg Snow knew. Harry knew, but I wasn't to know? I was the goat staked out to face that woman and I wasn't to know anything.'

'You were not staked out,' Kieran said, turning to her as her annoyance finally became obvious. 'I didn't want you worried. She might not have come here at all. I didn't want you on edge all the time.'

'You idiot,' Alissa shouted, hurling herself at him. 'The children could have been coming down the stairs with me, they could have heard everything.' She began to beat his chest with her fists, her face flushed, her hair wild about her head. 'I'm supposed to act without warning, face that witch without any sort of knowledge, and get ready to fight two big men who looked capable of breaking my neck?'

'Greg and Harry were there waiting just in case,' Kieran said hastily, dodging her blows and trying to restrain her.

'They're the best and I knew you'd be safe. I was on my way back when Greg phoned me.'

'Thanks for telling me at this late date,' she shouted, still trying to rain blows on his face.

He trapped her close and pinned her arms to her side, laughing down into her angry face. 'I admit there was a bit of risk with the children,' he said, still watching her warily, 'but I told them this morning they were not to come down until I came in and went up to see them.'

'So *they* knew and not me?' Alissa raged wildly, still struggling to inflict damage on him. 'Everybody knew but me!'

'They didn't know. I promised them a surprise if they kept in their rooms. I didn't really think she'd dare come here, actually arrive at the house,' he told her, trying to soothe with little hope of success. 'There was no real danger to either you or the children and I didn't want to worry any of you. I'm sorry if you had a fright but I'm glad Cynthia saw my wife in action, my beautiful, brave wife with long fair hair and a ferocity that could subdue a thousand dragons. I'm so proud of you, my darling. I would trust anything to you. I would trust my life to you.'

Alissa subsided slowly. 'You wanted to…to show me off to…to that woman?' Astonishment overcame her anger.

'I didn't plan it, but yes,' he confessed. 'I wanted her to see what a real woman looks like. I only wish I'd been here to see it for myself but they gave us the slip. I had to leave it to you and I knew I could.'

'I might have made a real hash of it,' Alissa muttered. 'I might have lost my temper and flown at her.'

'You're too clever for that,' Kieran said, smiling down at her. 'You only lose your temper with me. It's safe to fly at me because you know I love you.'

Her heart almost stopped. 'Do you, Kieran?'

'I've loved you since I first saw you. It was just a matter of capturing you and now it's a matter of keeping you.'

'I'll never go,' she whispered.

'I know, my love. I know.'

He held her more gently and looked into her entranced face, his gaze roaming over her wild beauty. The flush of temper had died from her cheeks but her eyes were glowing with happiness. 'I think you've forgiven me,' he ventured.

'I expect I always will – after a battle. Who was this acquaintance involved in the kidnap attempt?'

'A man called Bloomdale. He's a cheat and a liar. I've crossed swords with him before but this time I'll have to get serious. His money was behind this plot and I'll have to see to it that he has no money at all in future. He won't need money where he's going.'

He sounded ruthless and Alissa said, 'You're hard, aren't you?'

'Only with my enemies, not with my friends and not with the ones I love. And I love you, Alissa.'

Kieran kissed her lingeringly and then led her to the door, his arm round her waist.

'Let's tell the children they can come out now. I'll have to think of a good excuse for keeping them up there.'

'The surprise you promised would be nice,' Alissa pointed out. 'Or you could tell them they can now start going to school again, or you could tell them about the new baby.'

Kieran looked surprised. 'What new baby?'

'This one.' Alissa pulled his hand to her flat stomach. 'The time was right, in fact everything was right.'

'Oh, Alissa.' He folded her back into his arms. 'I'm keeping this as our secret for now. I don't want anyone else to know. I want to enjoy it just with you.'

'You're getting greedy, I see,' Alissa teased against his lips.

'I'm always going to be greedy about you. Get used to it. The children can go to buy some new toys. I'm keeping everything about you to myself.'

'Selfish,' she speculated.

'Happy,' Kieran corrected. 'Happy for the first time in my life. Maybe I'll be so happy that I'll lose my edge in business.'

'Automatons,' Alissa said, winding her arms round his neck, 'do not lose their edge. They just get re-programmed.'

'Right now I think I have been. I'm programmed to make love to you as often as possible.'

She tilted her head and looked at him. 'I'll see if I can fit you into my busy schedule. I'll have to draw up a plan but I expect it could be managed with a little thought.'

There were footsteps on the stairs and James burst in looking eager and excited. 'You're back. I could hear your voice. You promised a surprise.'

Kieran grinned down at him.

'Here's the surprise,' he said. 'How would you like a brother or a sister? There's a new baby on the way.'

James looked at Alissa and his eyes were alight.

'You're going to have a baby?'

'Brand new,' she told him.

He rushed across and gave her a hug. 'I'll be the oldest,' he said. 'There'll be a lot to teach this new baby. I'll get Sally.'

He raced out of the room and Alissa looked at Kieran with mocking surprise.

'My goodness. You blew it. I thought this was our secret, one you were keeping selfishly close to the chest.'

'I couldn't,' he laughed, grabbing her and dancing her round the room. 'I couldn't think of a thing but the wonderful news.'

'Are you happy?' she asked, her hand coming to touch his face.

'I'm delirious. How about you?'

'I'm dizzy. Will you stop swirling me around?'

He dropped into a chair and pulled her on to his lap, nuzzling his face against her neck.

'I've been thinking, in my mechanical way,' he murmured. 'I'm going to have all the doors fitted with special locks so that nobody can walk in and interrupt when I'm holding you. The idea is that they lock silently as we close the door and only open from the inside later. There'll be the necessary time lapse of course.'

'That's a very good idea,' Alissa said, wriggling closer. 'Obviously you have a first-rate brain.'

'Hmm. It's not something I would normally boast about.' They could hear the children coming down the stairs and he gave her a quick kiss. 'That will have to hold you until I get you in to bed. Now sit up and behave yourself.'

'Yes, sir,' Alissa said as the door burst open and the children launched themselves across the room.

'See what I mean about the locks?' Kieran muttered.

'I'll help you to fix them,' Alissa agreed, as she welcomed the children into her arms.

Romance at its best from Heartline Books™

We hope that you've enjoyed our latest selection of titles from Heartline Books. Over the coming months we will be offering you more new novels by both previously unpublished and experienced authors, containing stories with a dash of mystery, some which are tinged with humour and others high-lighting the passion and pain of love lost and rediscovered.

Our unique covers have been much admired and appreciated by our readers, capturing as they do evocative scenes such as a sleepy English town, an idyllic watermill and windsurfing off the coast of New Zealand.

Whatever the setting, you can be sure that our heroes and heroines will keep you enchanted and entertained for many hours.

Books we will be featuring in future months will include exciting stories, set in such glamorous locations as the steamy heat of the jungle, the sunshine coast of Australia and the dreaming spires of Oxford.

Why not tell all your friends and relatives about the exciting world of Heartline Books. They too can start a new romance with Heartline Books today by applying for their own, ABSOLUTELY FREE, copy of Natalie Fox's LOVE IS FOREVER.

To obtain their free book, they can:

- visit our website: www.heartlinebooks.com
- *or* telephone the Heartline Hotline on 0845 6000504
- *or* enter their details on the form below, tear it off and send it to:
  Heartline Books,
  FREEPOST LON 16243, Swindon, SN2 8LA

And, like you, they can discover the joys of subscribing to Heartline Books, including:

- ♥ A wide range of quality romantic fiction delivered to their door each month
- ♥ A monthly newsletter packed with special offers, competitions, celebrity interviews and other exciting features

Please send me my free copy of *Love is Forever*:

Name (IN BLOCK CAPITALS)

_____

Address (IN BLOCK CAPITALS)

_____

_____

_____

_____ Postcode _____

If you do not wish to receive selected offers
from other companies, please tick the box ☐

If we do not hear from you within the next ten days, we will be sending you four
exciting new romantic novels at a price of £3.99 each, plus £1 p&p. Thereafter,
each time you buy our books, we will send you a further pack of four titles.

Did you miss the first four exciting titles from Heartline
Books?

    SOUL WHISPERS by Julia Wild
    BEGUILED by Kay Gregory
    RED HOT LOVER by Lucy Merritt
    THE WINDRUSH AFFAIRS by Maxine Barry

If you did, then please write to us at:
    Heartline Books,
    FREEPOST LON 16243, Swindon, SN2 8LA

And we will despatch these books to you.

Heartline Books...

Romance at its best™